Spence meant to drop her at home and lea

He really did. He said less than a dozen words during the drive home, taking that time to admonish himself to slow down, cool off, remember that he wasn't interested in getting tangled up with a woman—*any* woman—right now. And especially not this one, who was trouble if he'd ever seen it. Too many strings, too many expectations, too many awkward circumstances. No matter how great it had felt to hold her in his arms, it was time to back off.

He thought he'd convinced himself. Until Libby turned to him at her door, gave him a smile that hit him like a punch in the stomach and lifted her face invitingly to his.

He kissed her because she seemed to expect him to. And then he kissed her because he wanted to. And then because he needed to. And then because he thought he'd die if he didn't.

Dear Reader,

The breakup of a marriage or long-term relationship often seems to leave deep scars that linger long after the broken heart has mended. "Once burned, twice shy" is a recurring theme in romance fiction, because it presents such a challenge for us as writers. Michael Spencer was definitely one of the most challenging heroes I've ever encountered!

Spence introduced himself to me one day as I was listening to Dan Seal's haunting song, "Everything That Glitters (Is Not Gold)". Beneath this lanky cowboy's sometimes surly exterior, I sensed his pain, his loneliness, his fear and his heartache. I fell hard for the guy—and for his young daughter. And I knew it would have to be a very special woman who could tempt him to take the enormous risk of falling in love again.

I spent weeks mentally "interviewing" potential heroines— an attorney, a doctor, a banker, a widowed mother of three—but none of them seemed quite right. Like Spence, I was beginning to wonder if this poor cowboy was going to have to ride off into the sunset alone. And then Libby Carter slipped into my mind...

Accompanied by a warmhearted grandmother and a menagerie of pets, Libby the veterinarian convinced me immediately that she was exactly the right woman to make Michael Spencer a very happy man. Next, all she had to do was convince him—and that was a bit more difficult for her. I hope you enjoy reading about their romance as much as I enjoyed watching it unfold on my computer screen.

Gina Wilkins

P.S. I love to hear from my readers.

Gina Wilkins
c/o Harlequin Temptation
225 Duncan Mill Road
Don Mills, Ontario, Canada
M3B 3K9

GOLD AND GLITTER
GINA WILKINS

Harlequin Books

TORONTO • NEW YORK • LONDON
AMSTERDAM • PARIS • SYDNEY • HAMBURG
STOCKHOLM • ATHENS • TOKYO • MILAN
MADRID • WARSAW • BUDAPEST • AUCKLAND

ISBN 0-373-25601-9

GOLD AND GLITTER

Printed in U.S.A.

1

MICHAEL SPENCER FINISHED his lukewarm coffee and gazed pensively through the dusty window of the quiet diner. He was looking out at everything he owned, all contained within a battered, twenty-four-foot motor home connected to an empty, badly dented one-horse trailer.

It wasn't a lot to have accumulated during the course of thirty-three years of hard living, he thought grimly.

Beneath the table, he kneaded the aching muscles of his right thigh. Only recently freed from a heavy hip-to-toe cast, the leg still felt weak and unfamiliar, and tended to stiffen whenever he sat in one position for too long.

The ten-year-old child sitting on the other side of the dull laminated tabletop squirmed restlessly and tugged at an ever-present baseball cap. "Dad? I'm still hungry. Could I have some pie?"

Spence dragged his gaze from that hauntingly empty trailer and signaled for the diner's only waitress. "Sure, Jamie. What kind do you want?"

"Chocolate, of course."

A smile tugged reluctantly at the corner of Spence's mouth. "Of course."

"Don't you want some, too?"

He shook his head. "Guess I'm not all that hungry today."

Jamie's skinny little shoulders slumped dejectedly.

Regretfully, Spence wished he was better at hiding his bad moods. Not that it would have done any good even if he managed to fake a grin; his precocious daughter could always read him like an open book.

Fifteen minutes later, he stood at the cash register beside the diner's exit, paying for two lunch specials and one slice of pie with what little remained of his winnings from the rodeo in Tucson two months ago. That was before the accident that had busted his leg, killed his horse and eaten up most of his savings.

Jamie stood behind him, looking through the glass door at the nondescript parking lot beyond. "Where are we, Dad?"

Spence couldn't remember the name of the town. He lifted a questioning eyebrow at the waitress, who now stood behind the register, serving as cashier. "Benton," she supplied, handing him change from his twenty-dollar bill. "Arkansas."

Jamie laughed. "I know what state we're in."

The formerly dour waitress suddenly smiled, a typical reaction to Jamie's infectious laugh. "Y'all have a nice day," she bade them as Spence turned toward the glass door.

A colorful, somewhat battered poster taped to the upper portion of the glass made him suddenly freeze. Four-inch letters blazed across the top of the poster, announcing, Coming To Little Rock: Tickets On Sale Now! The date for the concert was two weeks earlier; the poster should have been taken down by now. But it was the smiling face pictured beneath the words that had brought Spence to such an abrupt halt. He glared angrily into artfully made-up blue eyes that seemed to smile mockingly back at him.

Looking to see what had attracted Spence's attention, Jamie made a funny, quickly swallowed sound. "Let's go, Dad," she said, staring at the poster as though afraid it might come to life. "*Now,* okay?"

Spence looked down into the beseeching blue eyes turned up to him and reached out to shove the door open. A wave of stifling late-August heat washed over them. Limping across the threshold, he placed one hand on the child's shoulder as they walked side by side toward the RV that was the only home they had.

THEY MADE IT AS FAR as Little Rock—barely twenty miles from the diner—before the RV broke down. Parked on the narrow shoulder on the side of the busy Interstate 30, Spence looked under the hood, then closed his eyes and let a low, sibilant curse hiss from between his clenched teeth.

"Is it bad?" a quiet little voice asked from beside him.

Spence opened his eyes. "It's bad."

"What are we going to do?"

Wiping the back of one hand across his dripping brow, Spence stared blindly at the passing traffic and slowly shook his head. "I don't know, Jamie. I just don't know."

SPENCE FINGER COMBED his coffee-brown hair and checked to make sure his white cotton shirt was tucked neatly into the waistband of his faded jeans. He noticed that his scarred boots were dusty; he buffed them hastily on the legs of his jeans. Not the typical attire for a job interview, perhaps, but this was the best he had. And besides, he was applying for a position as a care-taker and maintenance man—hardly a vice president of anything.

He gave himself a moment to study the place where he hoped to work for the next few months. A sprawl-ing white frame farmhouse with black shutters and a full wraparound porch sat at the end of the long gravel driveway on which he stood. One of the black shutters hung crookedly, and there was a loose board on the porch just beyond the three steps he climbed to ap-proach the front door—which, he noted, could use a coat of paint. Huge flower beds surrounded the house, filled with flourishing bushes and flowers that were in need of some pruning and weeding.

Beyond the house lay some fifty acres of rolling pas-tureland, bordered by heavily wooded hills. A large barn and corral lay directly behind the house, and two horses, a big black and a smaller sorrel, grazed nearby. He glanced at the small, white-frame structure that sat behind and to the right of the main building. That must be the caretaker's cottage he'd been told about. There were no other houses within sight, though he'd passed several small ranches much like this one after turning off Highway 10 just west of Little Rock.

He'd caught a glimpse of a swimming pool behind the main house as he'd driven up, and he could see that there were several other large flower beds between the house and the cottage, which were connected by a brick walkway that was rapidly being overtaken by weeds.

The grass needed cutting and the fences looked as though they could stand some repair work.

Yeah, he thought with a nod of satisfaction. He could see that he was needed here. All he had to do now was convince the residents that he'd give them their money's worth—at least until he'd earned enough of their money to allow him to move on. Between his possible salary here and the insurance settlement he expected to receive within the next few months, he hoped there'd be enough to buy a new horse and trailer and get back on the rodeo circuit.

He needed this job. Badly.

He glanced at the dilapidated pickup he'd parked in front of the house. It wasn't much of a truck, but it was the best he could get when he'd traded in the ailing motor home and the dented horse trailer. At least it had gotten him this far. From her position in the passenger's seat of the truck, Jamie looked up from the book she was reading and gave him a thumbs-up sign of encouragement. He nodded in response and turned to knock firmly on the front door.

There was a clatter of noise from the other side of the door—a rhythmic thump-thump that grew steadily louder as it drew nearer—and then the knob turned. Spence found himself looking down into the piercing hazel eyes of a tiny gray-haired woman. She stood behind an aluminum walker, which explained the thumping noises he'd heard. "Mrs. Grandjean?" he asked, wondering if this was the woman to whom he'd spoken over the telephone earlier.

"Yes. You must be Mr. Spencer." Her voice was strong, not quavery as he might have expected from her rather fragile appearance. This was definitely the woman who'd extended the invitation for this interview.

"Yes, I'm Michael Spencer. I called you earlier about the caretaker position listed in the newspaper."

A glimmer of humor reflected in her lively eyes. "I remember why you called, Mr. Spencer. Why don't you come on in so we can talk about it. Who's that sitting in the truck?"

A bit disconcerted by her brusque manner, he glanced over his shoulder. "That's my daughter, Jamie. She'll be fine. She's reading."

"Well, don't leave her sitting out there. Tell her to come in and have some milk and cookies while we talk. She can read her book inside where it's cool."

"Oh, that's not—"

"I'll go pour her a glass of milk while you call her in." The woman turned with those words and thumped vigorously away, probably in the direction of the kitchen.

Spence shrugged slightly and turned to motion to Jamie. She looked surprised for a moment, then climbed out of the truck, her paperback book in hand. "What is it, Dad?" she asked as she hurried toward him.

"Mrs. Grandjean has invited you in for milk and cookies while she and I discuss the job. She said you can read inside where it's cool."

"That was nice of her."

"Yeah." He touched his daughter's shoulder. "Be on your best behavior, okay? I need this job."

Jamie rolled her eyes. "Like I'm going to start breaking up the furniture or anything."

He grinned. "Well, I thought it wouldn't hurt to warn you."

Mrs. Grandjean welcomed Jamie warmly into her home and settled her into a bright, clean, inviting kitchen with a glass of milk and a plate of what appeared to be home-baked cookies. Spence wasn't surprised when Jamie thanked the older woman politely and engagingly. His kid knew how to turn on the charm when it suited her, and he'd drilled proper manners into her. Mrs. Grandjean was thoroughly won over by the time she led Spence out of the kitchen for their interview.

Spence sent his daughter a wink and a way-to-go hand signal behind the woman's back as he left the room. Jamie grinned, picked up a cookie and opened her book again, settling happily into the world of the *Babysitter's Club*, mercifully unaware of quite how desperate their financial situation was at the moment. Which only made Spence all the more painfully aware of that grave situation.

In the den, Mrs. Grandjean went directly to an odd-looking upholstered chair that seemed to be leaning sharply forward. With a touch of a button, the chair lowered her slowly into a more natural sitting position. Spence assumed it would raise her up again when she was ready to stand. She motioned for him to be seated in a regular armchair close to her own. "Getting old is a pain in the lower anatomy, Mr. Spencer. Especially the hip—I fell and broke mine last spring. I'm still having some trouble with it."

"I'm sorry to hear that." He sat on the edge of the chair, stiffly at attention. He assumed that Mrs.

Grandjean had full authority to hire him or not, though she'd mentioned on the telephone that the property was actually owned by her granddaughter—who, she'd added proudly, was a local veterinarian. She'd also explained that their former caretaker had quit unexpectedly a few months earlier and that the two women were unable to keep up the place alone—Mrs. Grandjean because of her frail health, the granddaughter because of her busy work schedule.

"I noticed that you are limping rather badly yourself, Mr. Spencer. Have you injured yourself?"

"Broke my leg in a car accident a couple of months ago," Spence answered lightly. "It's healing just fine, but still a bit stiff. It won't stop me from doing the work that needs to be done around here."

She nodded. "You look strong enough."

"I am."

"You have experience with maintenance work?"

"Yes, ma'am. I've worked as a carpenter and a mechanic, and I've done plenty of odd jobs in my time."

"Gardening?"

"I know how to pull weeds, mow grass and spread fertilizer."

She smiled. "That covers most of it."

He returned the smile cautiously. "Yes, ma'am. Anything else I figure I can learn."

"Are you from Texas, Mr. Spencer?"

"I grew up in New Mexico. But I've spent the past few years on the road, traveling the rodeo circuit."

"Rodeo?" she repeated with interest. "How exciting. Do you win?"

He stifled a grin. "Sometimes."

"Your daughter travels with you?"

"Yes, ma'am. I've been a full-time single parent since she was five." He didn't particularly like talking about his personal affairs, but he figured the sympathy angle couldn't hurt. He needed this job even more for Jamie's sake than his own, and he didn't mind letting this woman know it.

"How does she attend school if you live on the road?"

"I've been home schooling her. I use the materials provided for children of migrant laborers. She's a bright kid, passes every standardized test with flying colors. She's even a little ahead of other kids her age." Suddenly aware that he was bragging, he fell silent.

Mrs. Grandjean's smile had deepened in response to his obvious pride in his daughter. "I could tell she's a very bright child. And so well behaved. You've done a good job with her, Mr. Spencer."

He actually felt his cheeks warm. He couldn't remember the last time anyone had complimented him so nicely on anything. "Thanks."

"You saw the little house next to this one?"

"Yes, ma'am."

"That's the caretaker cottage. If you work for us, you and Jamie would live there. A bus picks up the local children and takes them to a school a few miles down the road from here. Would you send Jamie to that school if you live here, or continue to educate her yourself?"

"I'd send her to school," Spence answered without hesitation. "She could use the interaction with other kids."

"Are you looking for a permanent position, Mr. Spencer, or are you just needing a temporary job until your leg heals enough to allow you to go back to the rodeo?"

Damn. Spence stiffened, knowing that this question was probably the most important she'd asked yet. He could lie—but he wouldn't. He didn't have much in the way of possessions, but he had his pride, and his honor. For Jamie's sake, he would probably sacrifice them both—but he hadn't gotten quite that desperate yet.

"I'm going to be honest with you, Mrs. Grandjean. I really want this job, and I'll give you your full money's worth if you hire me. I need time to heal, and money to get back on my feet financially. I lost my horse in the accident, and I need to find another one, then spend a few months working it, getting it ready for competition. If all goes well, I figure I'll be back on the road by the time school is out next spring."

The woman lifted an eyebrow in response to his candor, but he couldn't quite read her reaction. Had he just lost any chance at the position, or was he still in the running? He felt the muscles in his neck grow tighter. It wasn't that he couldn't find another job—he knew he could. But he couldn't imagine one that would be a more ideal setup for him and Jamie. This one came with a decent home, a kindly employer, a place for him to work a new horse and duties that would leave him free to find a second job for extra income. He held his breath as he waited for her to speak.

He wasn't expecting the question she asked. "How old are you, Mr. Spencer?"

"Thirty-three," he replied, wondering what that had to do with anything.

"Your rodeo days are growing rather limited, aren't they? I would assume that in rodeo, as in most other sports, the younger competitors have the edge."

Spence winced at the reminder of passing years—a reminder he hadn't needed. He was all too aware that he had to get back onto the circuit soon if he wanted to remain a serious competitor.

Noting his reaction, Mrs. Grandjean smiled sympathetically. "Forgive me for speaking so bluntly, but I have the advantage of my years, you see. You are still a young man, and I'm sure you are in good condition, other than your recent injury. I have no doubt that you can still compete if you choose. I suppose I'm simply curious about how much longer you plan to live the life of a rodeo gypsy."

He shrugged. "I don't know," he answered simply.

"I see." She studied him for several long, silent moments, during which Spence resisted the impulse to squirm beneath her inspection. "All right, Mr. Spencer, you may move into the cottage whenever you like. When you're ready to begin your work, just let me know and I'll tell you what we expect from you in the way of daily chores."

Spence stared at her. "I'm hired?"

She smiled. "Yes."

"Just like that?"

"Just like that."

"But, uh, don't you want references or, er, or something?" He knew he should leap to accept her offer of a job, but he was so startled by her abrupt decision that he found himself questioning his luck.

She looked intrigued. "Do you *have* references?"

"Uh, no, not really," he confessed. He supposed there were a few friends she could call who'd vouch for his honesty, but he didn't know what good that would do. They could tell her he was an adequate roper, but they knew nothing of any maintenance skills he might possess.

"Well, then. There's no need to waste time, is there?"

"But . . . well, shouldn't you check with your granddaughter? She may have some questions for me."

"Libby has entrusted me with hiring someone for this position, Mr. Spencer. She won't question my decision. She will, of course, probably have some instructions for you. I'm sure she'll discuss them with you when she has an opportunity."

"But—"

Mrs. Grandjean laughed softly. "Mr. Spencer, do you want the job or not?"

He grimaced ruefully. "I want it. And call me Spence. Everyone does."

"Fine. I answer to Emma—or Gran. Mrs. Grandjean is such a mouthful, isn't it?"

Spence allowed himself to relax a bit. For once, something had gone right for him. He just hoped to hell it didn't all come apart when the granddaughter came home. By now, he was so accustomed to being knocked down that he was always braced for the fall. But maybe, just this once, he'd hang on long enough to soften the landing a little.

LIBBY CARTER ENTERED the front door of her home with a weary sigh. She'd been in surgery all afternoon trying to remove an impacted kidney from a Labrador retriever that had died of cardiac failure after surviving a three-hour operation. Her entire body ached, and she was fighting the empty depression that always followed losing a family's beloved pet.

She pushed a short, dark blond curl out of her face and headed directly for the kitchen, from which issued appetizing aromas. This was one of those evenings when she was especially grateful that she had convinced her grandmother to move in with her when she'd bought this house and land a couple of years earlier. She couldn't bear the thought of coming home to an empty house after a day like this one.

"Gran? I'm home."

The tiny gray-haired woman standing at the stove turned with a bright smile. Her walker stood to one side, unneeded as Gran moved carefully around the conveniently arranged kitchen. "Hello, dear. Oh, goodness, you look exhausted. Rough day?"

"Very," Libby replied, leaning over to brush a kiss against her grandmother's soft, lined cheek. "How was yours?"

"Productive. I hired a new caretaker today."

"Already?"

"Yes. He's moving in tomorrow. He was the first to apply for the job. He's a very nice young man. You'll like him, I think."

"*Young* man?" Libby repeated, slowly closing the refrigerator door. "How young?"

"Four years older than you. Thirty-three. He's a single father, with an adorable ten-year-old daughter named Jamie. Wait until you meet her. She's a little sweetheart."

"Gran, are you sure he's aware of what we can pay? Even with the cottage provided, the salary isn't a great deal to offer a single father."

"He knows. I wouldn't be surprised if he moonlights a bit, which doesn't matter as long as he does everything around here first, does it?"

"Well, no, but—"

"His name is Michael Spencer. He's had experience with carpentry and maintenance work, and he's good with horses, which was another point in his favor. Wait until you see him. He even looks like a cowboy."

Libby bit her lip as she carried her soft drink to the table. Though she'd given her grandmother the authority to hire someone for the position, she had really expected to be consulted before Gran made a final decision. She'd thought there would be several applicants to consider, hadn't predicted that Gran would hire the first guy to come along. She sincerely hoped they weren't making a huge mistake. "I assume he had references?"

Gran cleared her throat. "Well, no. Not exactly."

"Oh, Gran—"

"He's a very nice man, Libby. I could tell as soon as I saw him with his little girl."

"I suppose the little girl is his reason for wanting a permanent position with a home provided," Libby mused, glancing through the kitchen window toward the caretaker's cottage.

"Well. . . ."

Something in her grandmother's voice made Libby wary. "What haven't you mentioned?"

"He isn't exactly looking for a permanent position. He's recovering from an accident, and he wants to get back into the rodeo circuit as soon as possible—probably by spring, he said. But he promised he would give us our full money's worth while he's here."

Libby thrust both hands into her tousled short curls, feeling a dull headache begin somewhere behind her temples. "Let me get this straight," she said. "You've hired a wounded stranger with no personal references and no evidence of his competence, a man who says himself that he'll be moving on no later than next spring, leaving us without help again. Is that right?"

Gran had the grace to look sheepish. "That pretty well sums it up," she admitted.

"Why?"

"He needed the job," her grandmother answered simply. "Once I saw that dear little girl, I couldn't turn them away. You'll understand when you meet them."

"I hope you're right." Libby dropped her hands, knowing that nothing would be gained by continuing this discussion. She would meet this Michael Spencer for herself before making any final decisions.

Gran patted Libby's shoulder. "Trust me, dear," she said. "I've never led you wrong so far, have I?"

"No," Libby had to admit. "Not so far."

Gran smiled. "And I haven't this time. Now how about dinner? I've made your favorite. Baked chicken with rice and fresh steamed vegetables."

Since there hadn't been time for lunch, Libby was ravenous. She knew full well that her favorite meal had been prepared to soften her reaction to Gran's surprise announcement, but it sounded too good to quibble right now. She moved toward the cabinets. "I'll set the table. We'll discuss this more after I meet the man, all right?"

Apparently confident that Libby would agree with her decision, Gran only smiled and turned back to the stove.

THE DAY AFTER being hired by Mrs. Grandjean, Spence sat in a wrought-iron spring rocker on the tiny brick patio behind the caretaker's cottage and watched Jamie frolicking with the big Irish setter and the feisty beagle who'd come to check out the new tenants. Jamie had always been crazy about animals—dogs, horses, cats, mice, goats, whatever. She'd been delighted to meet these two when they'd moved in a few hours earlier.

His gaze drifted, studying the place they would call home for the next few months. It was a nice spread, and the work wouldn't be that difficult. He and Jamie would do fine here for however long they stayed. He hoped to receive his insurance settlement from the accident in Tucson soon, which would allow him to buy a horse and start training it.

He thought sadly of Red Devil, the horse he'd owned before a drunken college kid had rammed into the side of the horse trailer behind Spence's motor home. Spence and Jamie had been uninjured, but Spence had sustained a badly fractured leg trying to free his hurting, panicked horse from the wreckage of the trailer.

Worse, Devil had been so badly wounded that they'd had to put him down. The week Spence had spent in a hospital bed cleaned him out financially.

Rodeo friends had taken care of Jamie until he was back on his feet. The college boy's insurance company had offered a settlement, but it hadn't been nearly enough to compensate for all Spence had lost. A hungry young lawyer had taken Spence's case, promising to get him a decent settlement.

He looked at the two horses grazing peacefully in the pasture behind the barn, and his fingers itched to hold a set of reins. Soon, he promised himself grimly. Soon.

A burst of laughter from Jamie brought his attention back to the child wrestling with the two friendly dogs. Spence smiled in response to the delighted sound. Yeah, he thought again. He and Jamie would be okay here. At least for a while.

"Mr. Spencer?"

The woman was standing at the end of the winding brick sidewalk that connected the main house to the cottage. Her dark blond hair was cut almost as short as his, framing her oval face in a cap of soft curls. She wore little makeup, if any, but her wide green eyes and full, soft mouth didn't need artificial enhancement. She looked young and fresh and congenial. Could this possibly be the veterinarian Mrs. Grandjean had spoken of so often and so proudly?

"Yes?"

"I'm Libby Carter," she said, answering his mental question.

Belatedly remembering his manners, Spence pushed himself to his feet. "Nice to meet you." He wondered if he should thank her for hiring him when it had actually been her grandmother who'd handled that task. Still, Mrs. Grandjean had explained that the granddaughter owned the place, so would technically be his employer. He looked her over a bit more carefully as she murmured a polite response.

She looked tired, he thought, studying the slight droop to her eyelids, the faint lines of weariness around her mobile mouth. He wondered why she'd felt it necessary to greet him on his first evening here. Being polite, or checking him out?

"We won't cause you any trouble," he assured her. "Your grandmother explained what needed to be done, and I've had experience with all of it. You'll get your money's worth, Dr. Carter."

She studied him for a moment, as if weighing his words against his appearance. He couldn't help wondering what she saw when she looked at him so seriously. And then she smiled again and held out her hand. "I hope you enjoy your stay here, Mr. Spencer."

She was a bit too slender and wholesome looking for his tastes, but she had a nice smile. He took her hand in his. "Thank you, Dr. Carter. I'm sure we will."

2

LIBBY HADN'T BEEN prepared for her initial reaction to Michael Spencer. Hadn't expected that the sight of his hard, tanned face and gleaming, inscrutable dark eyes would make her breath catch in her chest, her pulse start to race. Nor could she have known that the first touch of his hand on hers would make her heart jolt and her knees weaken.

What in the world was the matter with her? She'd never reacted like this to *any* man. And she didn't even know this one. So why was she suddenly finding it so very hard to breathe? Why did she find herself so utterly fascinated by his firm, beautifully shaped mouth?

Her hand lay limply in his as she stared at him, trying to think of something else to say. She must have been more exhausted this evening than she'd realized!

Two eager barks suddenly broke the spell that had momentarily fallen over her. A large shaggy body shoved against her, causing her hand to fall away from her tenant's. The big Irish setter rubbed adoringly against her, panting happily up at her. The stubby-legged beagle, not to be outdone, leaped at her side, trying to get high enough to claim her attention with his happy yaps.

Grateful for the distraction, Libby dropped her gaze to the dogs. "Hello, Sherman. Settle down, Peabody, I see you. Have you guys been making friends with our new neighbors?"

A grubby urchin in grass-stained jeans and a dusty baseball cap had followed the dogs to greet her. "Are these your dogs, ma'am?"

"Yes. This is Sherman," Libby said, patting the setter. "And that's Peabody," she added when the beagle barked demandingly.

The child laughed and tousled Peabody's droopy ears. "I like their names."

"Thank you." Libby studied the child as best she could, but the deepening dusk and the shadow of the baseball cap's brim made it difficult to see details other than a round face and a broad smile. Had Gran not told her that Michael Spencer had a daughter, Libby would have assumed this was a boy. "And what's your name?" she asked to make conversation, even though Gran had already told her.

"Jamie Spencer."

"It's nice to meet you, Jamie. I'm Libby Carter."

"Are you the vet Mrs. Grandjean told us about?"

"Yes, I'm a veterinarian."

"Cool. That's what I want to be when I grow up."

Libby smiled. "Is it?"

"Yep."

"Jamie," her father warned. "Remember your manners."

"Oh, sorry. I mean, yes, ma'am."

"And take off the cap," he added. "We can't even see your face."

Libby heard the faintest sigh of impatience, but the little girl obeyed without argument. A copper-colored ponytail tumbled out of the cap. Unshadowed now, a pair of bright blue eyes looked up at Libby, reflecting the smile that graced the child's round face. "Maybe I could ask you some questions sometime about your work?" she asked hopefully.

"Of course," Libby answered warmly. "You're welcome to come look over my clinic one day. I'll give you a personal tour of the facilities."

Jamie's eyes widened. "Really? Can I, Dad—I mean, may I? Please?"

"We'll see," her father replied, placing a hand on his daughter's shoulder. "You'd better go wash up now. You've gotten pretty grubby rolling around with those dogs."

"Okay. See you later, Dr. Carter."

"See you later, Jamie."

The back door closed with a bit too much force behind Jamie. Her father winced and looked rather apologetically at Libby.

"I'll talk to her about that. She won't tear the door off its hinges, or anything."

"I'm sure she won't. She's adorable."

"Thanks. She's a good kid." There was no mistaking the touch of pride in his deep voice.

Impulsively Libby asked, "Would you and Jamie like to join my grandmother and me for dinner, Mr. Spencer? We have plenty, and I'm sure you're tired after moving in today."

His smile faded. He shook his head, the movement ruffling the coffee-brown hair tumbled across his forehead. "Thank you, but no. Jamie and I picked up take-out earlier. We'll just heat it in the microwave and then turn in early."

Libby sensed that he was turning down more than this one impromptu invitation. He seemed to be making it quite clear that he wasn't interested in socializing with his employers.

She pushed her hands into the pockets of her khaki slacks and took a step backward, almost stumbling over Sherman. "Fine," she said. "Please let Gran or me know if you need anything. She's here all day, and I'm home most evenings."

He nodded.

Feeling suddenly awkward and self-conscious, Libby turned away. "Good night, Mr. Spencer."

"G'night."

She could sense him watching her as she called her dogs to follow and headed down the path toward her house. It took an effort to keep her steps slow and unhurried, when what she really wanted to do was get out of his sight as quickly as possible.

SHE ENTERED HER HOUSE through the back door into the kitchen. Her grandmother looked up from the pans bubbling on the stove. "Did you meet them?"

"I met them," Libby replied, keeping her expression bland.

"Well? What did you think?"

"Jamie seems like a sweet child."

"And Spence?"

Libby had called him Mr. Spencer. He hadn't suggested anything different to her. She lifted the lid from one of the pans and took an appreciative sniff of the vegetable soup stewing inside. "What about him?"

"What did you think of him?" Gran asked, her softly rounded body practically quivering with impatience.

Libby couldn't imagine why her grandmother was so determined to discover her reaction to Michael Spencer, but she shrugged and answered. "He seemed okay. I don't think he'll give us any trouble. At least, I hope he won't."

"I'm sure he won't," Gran replied, though she sounded a bit disappointed with Libby's lukewarm response. "He seems like a very nice young man."

Libby didn't reply. She was still stinging a bit from that "nice young man's" firm rebuff of her dinner invitation.

Gran made a face and shook her head. "You must be starving," she said suddenly, moving back to the stove. "Go wash up and I'll get the food on the table. You can tell me all about your day during dinner."

Libby found it rather amusing that Gran used the same tone with her that she'd heard in Michael Spencer's voice when he'd sent his ten-year-old daughter inside to wash up. Some things would never change, she mused.

She washed her hands and face in the bathroom connected to her bedroom, then reached for a comb, her thoughts still centering on her oddly powerful reaction to Michael Spencer. She could still clearly picture his lean, weathered face, his rather shaggy dark hair, his slim, strong-looking body. Even had it not been for his denim shirt, faded jeans and well-worn western boots, she would have pegged him as a cowboy—the kind who broke women's hearts as easily as he made them flutter.

She remembered the almost physical jolt she'd received when her eyes had first met his. Dark, glittering, rather angry eyes, filled with old ghosts and seething emotions she couldn't begin to identify. Who was this man? And why had she turned to jelly when he'd looked at her?

Her mouth twisted as she mentally answered her own question. She knew full well what her racing pulse and weakened knees had signified. She was old enough and experienced enough to recognize the symptoms of immediate, powerful attraction—maybe even a touch of good, old-fashioned lust. It had never hit her quite that strongly before, but she'd taken one look at Michael Spencer and all but drooled. How foolish of her. She was almost thirty, far too old to behave like a starry-eyed schoolgirl at the sight of a sexy cowboy.

Particularly a sexy cowboy who'd shown absolutely no sign of experiencing even the slightest attraction in return.

She gazed pensively at the reflection staring back out at her from the mirror over the sink. Her hair was still tousled from a hard day at work, and the makeup she'd applied that morning had long since worn off, leaving her too-short nose shiny and her cheeks rather pale from weariness. Her lashes were dark enough not to disappear without mascara, but there was nothing exotic or mysterious about her wide-set, round green eyes. Deep dimples pushed into her cheeks when she smiled, and she'd long since grown tired of being told how "cute" and "sweet" they made her look. The body beneath her practical forest-green T-shirt and khaki slacks was as slim and supple as a young boy's—and just about as sexy, she thought with a sigh.

She looked at the comb clutched in her capable, callused hands with their short, unpainted nails. And she reminded herself that she was perfectly content with who she was, what she did and how she looked. It was stupid to let one man's lack of interest shake the self-confidence she'd spent a lifetime developing. Even if he did make her knees go weak when he looked at her.

Shaking her head in exasperation, she dropped the comb on the countertop with a clatter and snapped off the bathroom light. Gran was waiting for her, and she was hungry. It was time to put Michael Spencer out of her mind and get back to her own completely satisfactory life.

SOMETIME DURING THE NIGHT, Spence crawled out of the double bed in the bedroom he'd claimed, and walked silently through the darkened living room to the back door. Wearing only a pair of jeans, he stepped out onto the patio, drawing a deep breath of the still-warm night air. A canopy of stars spread above him, and an almost-full moon provided illumination without color. Crickets and frogs sang loudly from the woods and pastures, and the muffled snorting of a horse drifted from the corral. Far in the distance, a dog barked.

The main house was dark and quiet, its residents probably long asleep. As he would have been had the erotic dream not awakened him, leaving him hard and aching and frustrated. He didn't remember any of the details of the dream, but he knew who'd shared his bed in his sleep world.

Delilah. Copper-haired, blue-eyed Delilah, with her voluptuous body and oh-so-damned-clever mouth and hands.

He wondered where she was tonight. He wondered what poor, lucky fool was receiving the benefit of her sensual talents. And he wondered if he—or their daughter—ever crossed her single-track mind.

He'd quit smoking several years ago, to set a good example for Jamie, but tonight he longed for a cigarette almost as fiercely as he ached for a woman.

"Damn you, Delilah," he muttered, glaring at the moon that glowed as brightly as the avaricious gleam in Delilah's restless eyes. "Damn you, wherever the hell you are."

MORE THAN A WEEK PASSED before Libby saw either of the Spencers again, except in passing as she drove her Ford Explorer out of the driveway early in the mornings or back sometime after six every evening. It was an extremely busy time for her and her partner, Paul Baker. Theirs was a small-animal practice, mostly cats and dogs, and business was thriving. Which was nice financially, but murder on a social life.

Taking advantage of a free hour Friday evening for a lazy, after-dark swim, Libby floated on her back, her mouth twisting as the phrase repeated in her mind. Social life? *What* social life? She could hardly even remember the last time she'd been on a date. Which might explain why the memory of Michael Spencer had haunted her for the past few days.

Her grandmother had spent quite a bit of time with him during the past week, showing him around and explaining his duties, and still seemed as taken with him as she'd been the first day. He'd gotten a fair start already on the most pressing repair work. And he was doing a good job, too, as Libby had noticed for herself. He'd even fixed the broken stall door that Libby had been meaning to get to as soon as she had time.

Gran had said that little Jamie was never out of her father's sight, tagging at his heels as he worked around the place, cheerfully serving as his assistant. Jamie had already befriended both the dogs and the horses, and Gran was besotted with the child. Libby only hoped Gran wouldn't get too attached; Michael Spencer had made it very clear that he didn't intend to stay long.

A rustling from the azalea bushes lining the pool made Libby drop her feet to the bottom of the pool and turn quickly in that direction. "Sherman?" she said, hoping it was only her dog spying on her.

There was a startled squeak, and then a pale little face peeked over the top of the bushes. "Dr. Carter?" Jamie asked tentatively.

Libby waded to the side of the pool. "Yes. Are you out here alone, Jamie? It's almost ten o'clock."

Jamie stepped out of the bushes onto the concrete patio that surrounded the pool. "Yes, ma'am. I'm not supposed to come out at night, but I suddenly remembered that I left my sunglasses out here when Dad and me were working on the pool pump this morning. I was afraid one of the dogs would find them and chew them up."

Libby crossed her arms on the side of the pool. "Do you see them?"

Jamie looked around, then pounced on something lying in one of the chaise longues grouped invitingly around the pool area. "Here they are!" she said, holding them up.

In the soft, artificial illumination of the patio lights, Jamie's loosened, shoulder-length red hair glowed and her fair skin took on a translucent sheen. She was a pretty child, Libby mused, even in the tomboy T-shirts and cutoffs she seemed to favor. Not that Libby blamed her for that; she preferred comfortable, practical clothing herself. "Your dad knows you're out here, I hope. He'll be worried if he can't find you."

"Dad's working at his other job tonight," Jamie explained. "He won't be home until late—three in the morning, maybe."

"You aren't home by yourself, are you?" Libby asked, starting to frown. Surely the man had hired a sitter if he was moonlighting on the night shift.

"Well, yeah—I mean, yes, ma'am. Like I said, I'm not supposed to go out after dark, but I wanted to find my sunglasses. But it's okay, I'll hurry right back home and lock all the doors, just the way I'm supposed to."

There was no way Libby approved of leaving a ten-year-old child alone in a house all night—not even a child as well behaved as this one apparently was. "Why don't you stay at my house tonight, Jamie?" she suggested. "We'll leave a note for your father, telling him where you are."

Jamie's eyes grew wide. "Oh, no, ma'am. Um, thank you, but I couldn't do that. Dad wouldn't let me stay over without asking him first."

Libby planted both hands on the concrete pool skirting and hoisted herself out of the water. "All right. Then I'll come stay with you. You can go on to bed, and I'll sit up and read until your dad comes home. I'd like to talk to him."

"But I'm not supposed to let anyone in the house when Dad's not home," Jamie protested, looking worried now.

Libby smiled, trying to look nonthreatening. She didn't want to upset the child, but she wasn't about to leave her alone overnight. If it disturbed Jamie too badly to disobey her father's orders about visitors, Libby would sit on the front porch until Michael Spencer arrived home.

Still, she tried one more time. "It's not as if I'm a stranger, Jamie. I'm your neighbor."

"You're not going to yell at my dad about anything, are you?" Jamie asked suspiciously.

"Of course not." Libby resisted an impulse to cross her fingers behind her back. She had no intention of yelling at the man, but she did have a few pointed things to say to him. "I just haven't had a chance to talk to him this week. I want to thank him for all the work he's done around here." *Among the other things I intend to discuss with him.*

"Oh." Jamie thought about it a moment, then shrugged. "It *is* your house. If you want to wait for my dad, then I guess it's okay."

"Thank you, Jamie. And I'll take full responsibility, okay?"

Jamie only shrugged again, as if uncertain what to say. And then she suddenly stiffened. "I'd better get back in the house. Dad always calls at ten o'clock to tell me good-night and make sure I'm okay."

"Then hurry back inside," Libby urged her. "He'll worry if you don't answer. I'll change and be along in a few minutes."

With a nod and a flip of her hair, Jamie turned and sprinted for the cottage.

Beginning to frown again, Libby hurried into her own house, water dripping from her as she walked. She ignored the damp trail behind her, taking the back stairs up to her bedroom, where she stripped off the wet bathing suit, dumped it in the tub and ducked her head in the sink to rinse out the chlorine. Leaving her hair to dry naturally, she dressed quickly in shorts and a knit shirt and slid her feet into a pair of white huaraches. And then she snatched the hardcover book off her nightstand and headed back downstairs.

Gran was in the kitchen, having her usual cup of cocoa before turning in. She looked up in surprise. "You're going back out?"

In as few words as possible, Libby explained. "Don't wait up for me," she added. "It's going to be very late."

Gran was frowning now, too. "I'm surprised that Spence would leave the child alone like this. He's so devoted to her, watches her every minute when they're together. He must think she's capable of taking care of herself, or he'd never risk leaving her alone at night."

"Gran, she's a ten-year-old child! Even the most mature ten-year-old is too young to be alone until three in the morning."

Her grandmother sighed. "I know. Of course, this is really none of our business. . . ."

"They're living in my cottage," Libby answered flatly. "That makes me responsible if anything goes wrong—which makes this my business."

"Still," Gran murmured, wringing her work-roughened hands, "you will try to be tactful, won't you? If you make him angry, he'll probably just pack up and leave, and I'd hate to see that happen. There are still so many things to be done—and Jamie seems so happy here."

Libby shook her head and swallowed a sigh of her own. Gran was getting too attached, she thought regretfully. She'd been afraid of this—but she'd thought it would take more than a week!

She'd really hate to see Gran hurt when the Spencers moved on. Libby had no intention of becoming that fond of the temporary handyman and his child, despite her quite natural concern for Jamie's safety.

"I'd better get on over there," she said, tucking her book under her arm and grabbing a diet cola out of the refrigerator on her way past. "Jamie should be in bed."

"Remember, Libby—be diplomatic," Gran called out one last time as Libby opened the back door and stepped outside. Libby noted that her grandmother didn't sound overly optimistic.

SPENCE MUFFLED A GROAN as he climbed out of the battered truck. He'd traded the RV and trailer for the truck—and knew full well he'd gotten the short end of the deal. Not that he'd had a hell of a lot of choice. He just hoped he could come up with a down payment on another RV before spring—and after tonight, that was looking less likely all the time.

Carrying his dusty western hat in one hand, he pressed the other to his bleeding mouth as he limped toward the front door of the cottage. He noted the light shining through the living room window; Jamie would be in bed, of course, but she always left a light on for him.

God, he was tired. Body and soul tired. If it weren't for Jamie, damned if his life would be worth living.

He'd taken two shuffling steps into the living room when he realized that someone was sleeping in his chair.

3

SPENCE RUBBED his tired eyes to make sure he was seeing clearly. He'd taken a couple of blows to the head tonight, but he wasn't hallucinating. For some reason, Libby Carter was sound asleep in the brown plaid recliner that matched the other neat, inexpensive furnishings provided with the cottage. A hardcover novel lay in her lap, still open to the page she'd been reading when she'd fallen asleep. Her head rested against the back of the chair, and her unpainted face looked soft and lightly flushed. Her lips were slightly parted, and again he thought what a nice mouth she had.

And then he wondered what the hell he was doing standing in the middle of his living room floor, staring at a sleeping woman. What was she doing here?

Had something gone wrong?

His heart suddenly leaping to his throat, Spence moved swiftly across the room toward Jamie's closed bedroom door, ignoring the protest of his bad leg. He found his daughter sleeping peacefully in her bed, illuminated by the glow of the night-light plugged into an outlet near the floor. Touching her soft little face with a hand that was suddenly not quite steady, he reassured himself that she seemed fine, no fever or outward injuries.

He exhaled deeply in relief.

He moved back into the living room and approached the recliner warily, wondering how to go about waking Libby. He didn't want her to scream or anything and frighten Jamie. He touched her shoulder. "Miss, uh, Dr. Carter?"

She frowned, blinked, then sat bolt upright. Her cheeks darkened. "Oh, no. I went to sleep, didn't I?"

He stepped back. "Yeah. You want to tell me what you're doing here?"

She made an effort to pull herself together by running a hand through her hair and rising to her feet—which, he noted, were bare. A pair of sandals lay tumbled on the floor beside the chair. Her voice was still a bit husky when she spoke. "I wanted to talk to you about—"

And then she stopped, and her eyes widened as they focused on his face. "What happened to you?"

He grimaced and self-consciously touched his swelling right eye and split lip. "A little altercation at work," he muttered.

"Just what kind of work do you do?" she demanded, hands on her slender hips. "Prizefighting?"

"I'm a bouncer for a bar downtown—or at least," he added glumly, "I *was* a bouncer. I got fired tonight. The manager didn't like the way I handled the trouble that developed. Seems I offended one of his best-paying regular customers by stepping into his fist."

"Well, don't expect me to tell you I'm sorry," Libby said frankly. "That sounds like a terrible job. And what were you thinking of, leaving Jamie alone at all hours of the night?"

Spence's hand dropped abruptly to his side. He narrowed his eyes. "That 'terrible job' paid damned well, and I need the money," he said. "As for my decisions about my daughter—they're no one's business but my own."

"I'm aware of that," Libby replied, and her voice was cool. "I'm not questioning your competence as a father, Mr. Spencer, but I don't think a ten-year-old should be left at home alone at night. Too many things could go wrong—fire, or accidents, or break-ins. This is a quiet neighborhood, and we've had little trouble, but one never knows what could happen."

"You think I don't know that?" Spence returned, shoving a hand through his hair. "You think I liked leaving her here by herself? I didn't. But I have to support her somehow, and while the lodging and salary you're providing for the caretaker job come in handy right now, it's not enough alone. I've been asking around for someone to come sit with her, but so far I haven't had any leads on a night-shift sitter."

It galled him to have to explain himself and his actions after being on his own for so long. He certainly didn't owe this woman any explanations—and he wouldn't be giving any had he not been fighting a guilty suspicion that she was right about his lack of judgment in leaving Jamie alone. Damn it.

Libby looked thoughtful. "I can understand that," she said finally. "I have nothing against you taking another job—you've certainly been doing everything I could ask around here. In fact, if you could find a daytime job, I'm sure you could do any chores around here in the afternoons and on weekends. If you must work nights, Jamie can sleep in the main house with Gran and me. There's no need for you to hire a baby-sitter when we're right here."

"I'm not going to take advantage of you like that," Spence argued. "I'll find someone—maybe I'll put an ad in the paper."

"And hire some stranger to take care of your daughter?" Libby shook her head. "No telling what kind of nut you'd end up with. You wouldn't be taking advantage of us by letting Jamie stay over. We have plenty of extra rooms, and Jamie would be no trouble at all. I have to go out on call some nights, but Gran rarely goes out in the evenings. One of us is almost always at home.

"Besides," she added with a slight smile, "in case you haven't already noticed, my grandmother is besotted with your child. If she'd known about your problem, she would have already made this offer, I assure you."

Spence could feel his jaw clench with his chagrin at finding himself in this position. "This is all academic, anyway," he muttered, avoiding her eyes. "I don't even have a night job now, remember?"

"I know. But if you find another one, you'll let Jamie stay with us?"

"I'll think about it."

She smiled. "Good. So what sort of job will you be looking for now? Maybe I can help."

He balled his fists and placed them on his hips, pride kicking his chin higher. "I can find my own jobs."

She sighed gustily, then stifled a yawn, reminding him that they were having this conversation in the middle of the night—near dawn, actually. "You really are a pigheaded cowboy, aren't you?" she asked in a matter-of-fact tone. "I've lived in this area all my life. I know a lot of people. I have some contacts. There's a chance I could lead you to someone if you'd only let down that macho ego of yours enough to give me a few clues about what sort of job experience you have."

She was making him feel stupid for resisting when he'd just said he needed an extra paycheck. He didn't want to take any favors from her—but damn it, a job was a job. "I've been on the rodeo circuit for the past five years," he admitted. "Haven't made the big time, but I've done okay until an accident temporarily side-lined me a few months back."

She glanced down at his legs, proving that she'd no-ticed the slight limp he still retained from that acci-dent. "So you know horses."

"I know horses. I've worked as a ranch hand, and a trainer. Trained my own roping horses," he added, ruthlessly ignoring the catch of sadness when he thought of Red Devil.

Her eyebrows lifted. "Yeah? You any good?"

"Lady, I'm damned good," he drawled, and waited for her to flush at the innuendo. He figured he de-served a bit of retribution for the unrequested scolding she'd given him.

She didn't even blink. Either she didn't catch it, or she ignored it. "I know some horse owners who are look-ing for good trainers. As a matter of fact, I've been thinking about hiring one myself. Tennessee, the black gelding, is barely saddle broken. He's two and a half, plenty old enough for training, and I've been meaning to get started, but I just don't have the time. I usually ride Alabama, the sorrel mare, and lead Ten behind us when I've got a little extra time."

"What sort of training do you want for him?" Spence asked. "You planning to show him? Rope? Cut? Barrel race?"

She chuckled and shook her head, and he noted again that she looked tired. "Nothing like that. I just wanted another good recreational riding horse trained for neck reining. I like to ride through the woods when I get a few hours away."

Spence nodded. "No problem."

She studied him. "But you could train him for any of those other things you mentioned?"

"I've been watching him the past week. He's a good horse. Given a little time, I could train him to do anything you wanted." Spence wasn't bragging, just stating facts. He might have a lousy track record with people, but he was damned good with horses. Anyone who knew him—even those who disliked him—would admit that.

"Tomorrow's Saturday," Libby said unnecessarily. "I've got the day off. Let's meet at the barn tomorrow afternoon, after we've both gotten some sleep, and talk about it. You do a good job with Ten, and I'd be happy to recommend you to those other horse owners I mentioned. There's plenty of work for you around here if you're as good as you say you are."

A chance to work with horses again. Beats the hell out of trying to corral drunks in a crowded, smoky bar. Spence cleared his throat and looked down at his boots. "All right. And, uh, thanks," he added rustily.

She shrugged. "You've got to prove you know what you're doing first. I don't make recommendations on faith." And then she yawned again. "I'm going to get some sleep. You'd better do the same."

He nodded. He thought about thanking her for keeping an eye on Jamie—he sensed that she'd done so out of genuine concern for the child's safety—but he decided he'd thanked her enough. After all, she had been pretty arrogant about butting into his personal business. No need to get carried away with this gratitude bit.

Libby paused in front of him on her way to the front door. She touched his swollen lip with the tip of one finger. "You might try a cold pack on that to bring down the swelling."

Before he could react, she was gone. Spence blinked bemusedly at the door she'd closed quietly behind her, then shook his head.

Damned if he could get a handle on that one, he thought. One minute she was chewing him out, the next she was briskly offering assistance as if they were old friends. Why? Because she was a genuinely nice, helpful person? Because of Jamie? Or was there another reason behind her helpfulness?

There hadn't been any flirtatiousness in her manner toward him, though he had grown rather accustomed to receiving attention from women who seemed to find his emotional distance a challenge. If she was particularly attracted to him, she certainly didn't show it. Which, he thought, was just as well. She wasn't his type.

Nice mouth, though.

He felt his sore lip again, his fingers lingering at the spot she'd touched so lightly. And then he headed for the kitchen for an ice pack. He needed some sleep. Maybe after he was rested he'd be better prepared to deal with the puzzling Dr. Libby Carter.

LIBBY WAS SO TIRED she was aching when she finally climbed into her bed. She expected to fall asleep the minute her head hit the pillow. Instead, she found herself drifting in a state of semiconsciousness, remembering the way Michael Spencer had looked, battered and weary and stubbornly proud in his tight-fitting jeans and slant-heel boots. It had been all she could do to speak coherently, though she hoped she'd managed to hide her reaction from him.

The man was an enigma. Good worker, apparently devoted father, but stubborn as a mule and almost defiantly independent. She'd seen animals that had been mistreated who displayed much the same wary distrust of people that she'd noticed in Michael Spencer. Who had hurt him so badly? His family? Jamie's mother? Both?

She'd always been drawn to those who needed her. Even the biggest, strongest animals were vulnerable— though often dangerous—when they were in pain, and she could never resist trying to help. Like the wounded animals she treated, Spence was likely to snap at a hand outstretched to him, but she still felt as though she should try.

She was probably being a damned fool, she thought as she sank more deeply into her pillows. But she'd worry about that tomorrow.

IT WAS IMMEDIATELY apparent to Libby the next afternoon that Spence had a special affinity for horses. The way he talked to them, the way he touched them, even the way he looked at them, told her that his love and respect for horses were deep and genuine. He quickly had her mare, Alabama, literally eating out of his hand. Libby watched wryly as her horse flirted with him like a shameless hussy, as taken by this cowboy's lazy charm as Libby had been herself. Tennessee was almost as bad, standing back just long enough to remind everyone that he was a tough male, then eagerly sidling up for a piece of the carrot Spence offered so casually.

Libby couldn't help wondering if Spence was aware of this magnetism he had for the animals, and—damn it—for her.

She stayed out of the way and watched as Spence saddled Tennessee, who gave only token resistance to the procedure. Libby had saddled the horse several times, and had sat on his back a time or two, but knew the animal was far from being well trained. She simply hadn't had the time to work with him.

"Given enough time, Dad will have that horse toe dancing and doing pirouettes," Jamie drawled in an amusingly grown-up tone. She stood on the bottom rail of the fence next to Libby, her arms crossed on the top rail, her baseball cap pulled low over her round little face as she watched her father handling the horse. Libby's dogs wrestled on the ground behind them, staying close to their new ten-year-old best friend.

Libby smiled, wondering whom Jamie was quoting about her father's horse-training talents. "Just so he doesn't dress him up in a tutu. I don't think Ten would care much for that."

Jamie giggled. "Dad won't do that," she assured her. "He hates it when people make their horses look silly."

"So do I. Do you like horses, Jamie?"

"Yes, ma'am. I'm going to barrel race soon as I'm a little bigger and Dad can afford to buy me a horse. I've already tried a few times and I'm pretty good for my age." She made the comment with totally unselfconscious candor. As far as Jamie was concerned, she was stating a fact, not bragging. Libby thought the child was very much like her father.

Resting an elbow on the fence, Libby turned to fully face Jamie. "Do you like living here so far, Jamie?"

"I like it here a lot," Jamie replied, her bright blue eyes gleaming with sincerity. "It's nice living in a real house instead of a motor home for a change."

Libby wondered about Jamie's life on the road with her rodeo-following father. Was the child happy without permanent friends? Did she spend many hours alone? Did she know what she was missing by not having a real home, not having a mother or siblings, not being in school with other children her age? Did she ever see her mother, or any other family members, or was Spence the only family she had?

Knowing that none of those questions was any of her business, Libby kept them to herself. Instead, she asked, "Gran said your dad enrolled you in school this past week. You'll be starting in a couple of weeks, won't you? Are you looking forward to it?"

Jamie's smile faded noticeably. "School starts a week from next Monday," she agreed. "And I guess it'll be okay."

"You don't sound very certain."

Jamie plucked gravely at a large splinter sticking out from a fence rail, the action allowing her to avoid Libby's eyes. "I like it when Dad teaches me my lessons," she said. "I've been to a few schools—two in kindergarten and three in first grade—but I didn't like them much. That's when Dad started teaching me, after one of his women rodeo friends told him that's what she does with her kids."

Libby pushed aside her questions about Spence's "women rodeo friends." Instead, she tried to encourage Jamie. "I'm sure you'll enjoy being in school here," she said bracingly. "You'll be in, what, fourth grade?"

"Fifth."

"Even better. You'll have lots of field trips and fun school projects."

Jamie murmured something noncommittal.

It occurred to Libby that Jamie might be less anxious about starting school if she could first meet some of her classmates. Libby knew several families within the area with children close to Jamie's age. She opened her mouth to suggest that she arrange introductions, then closed it abruptly when she realized that she should probably discuss the matter with Spence first. While she couldn't imagine any reason for Spence to object, Libby had no right to make plans for his daughter without consulting him first.

She turned back to watch Spence, who'd been leading Tennessee with the reins, talking in a low voice to the wary animal, soothing him before attempting to mount. When he judged that the horse was ready, Spence slid his left boot into the stirrup and lifted himself cautiously upward. Tennessee moved restlessly.

Spence swung his right leg over the saddle in one smooth, practiced move, gathering the reins in his left hand, on which he wore a battered leather glove. Tennessee started to dance—a few quick steps to the right, a small leap to the left, a few sliding moves backward. Spence rode him easily, talking in a low, easy voice the entire time, patting the horse's neck with his right hand while he held the reins firmly with his left.

Libby felt her mouth go dry. There was just something about this man that turned her into a mass of raging hormones. She could stand here for hours just watching him, mounted on the gleaming black horse. No man had ever looked more right to her than Spence did in his well-worn black western hat with its silver concho band, a faded denim shirt with the sleeves rolled up on his forearms, washed-soft, glued-to-his-lower-body jeans and scarred, unpretentious western-heeled boots. It was more than ninety degrees today, and sweat gleamed on his bruised face and made dark patches on his shirt. Some men would have looked like accountants dressed up for Halloween in that outfit; Spence looked like the lean, tanned, long-legged cowboy he was.

"Dr. Carter?" Jamie said, and something about her tone made Libby suspect it wasn't the first time the child had said her name.

Fighting a blush, Libby cleared her throat. "What is it, Jamie?"

"Gran said it would be okay if I went swimming in your pool this afternoon."

"Yes, of course, as long as an adult is there to watch you," Libby agreed immediately. "Have you asked your dad yet?"

"Yes, ma'am. He said it was okay, and that he'll watch me. I just wondered if maybe you'd come swim with me," she said a bit shyly. "It would be more fun having someone to swim with."

Libby smiled. "I'd love to swim with you, Jamie."

Jamie grinned happily. "Great."

The child really was lonely, Libby thought again. Though Jamie obviously adored her father, she needed feminine company, her own age and older. Libby hadn't missed noting Jamie's use of the name "Gran." She was sure her grandmother had invited Jamie to call her that.

She couldn't help worrying again that Gran—and even Jamie, perhaps—were getting too attached, starting to imagine relationships that weren't real and couldn't last. Libby would hate to see anyone get hurt when Spence grew restless and finally moved on. She had to keep that inevitability in mind—for her grandmother's sake, and for her own.

LIBBY PULLED ON her most modest swimsuit, a sensible black tank, and topped it with a short black-and-white kimono. She'd promised to meet Jamie at the pool in ten minutes. She'd told Spence that there was no need for him to play lifeguard, since she would watch over Jamie. He'd only nodded and gone back to his chores, which Libby had taken to be an assent.

She was taken completely unaware when she stepped out her back door and found Spence standing beside the pool, wearing nothing but a snug-fitting pair of dark blue swim trunks. He was tanned and lean, his chest covered by a light mat of hair, his shoulders broad and sleek, his stomach taut, legs long and lanky. Even though she couldn't help noticing that he seemed to have a lot of old scars scattered over his body, she thought he looked wonderful.

She somehow managed not to fall over her own feet. Her smile felt forced. "You've decided to join us."

"Yeah. A swim sounded pretty good, as hot as it is today. You don't mind, do you?"

"Of course not." Libby turned to Jamie, who danced impatiently nearby, dressed in a red-white-and-blue swimsuit, her copper ponytail bouncing behind her. "Can you swim, Jamie?"

"Yes, ma'am. Want me to show you?"

"Of course."

Jamie hopped onto the low diving board and jumped into the water in a classic cannonball position. The resulting splash liberally dampened both Libby and Spence, who'd been standing close to the edge. Jamie came up grinning and paddling energetically toward the side of the pool. "How was that?" she asked.

Spence wiped a drop of water off his chin. "You're going to have to pay for that, you know," he drawled.

Jamie squealed happily and struck out quickly toward the other side of the pool.

Spence dove into the water with hardly a ripple. He caught up easily with his daughter, and a noisy, wet, enthusiastic water fight ensued. Libby stood watching, smiling, but feeling rather superfluous. The bond between father and daughter was strong, and exclusive. Libby wondered if they would ever allow anyone else to get truly close to them.

"Help, Dr. Carter!" Jamie called out, surfacing near Libby with a broad grin. "He's bigger than I am. You're not just going to stand there and watch him drown me, are you?"

"No, I won't watch that," Libby replied, straight-faced.

"Whew!" Jamie giggled in relief.

"I'll turn my back so I can't see," Libby added, then proceeded to do so.

"Dr. Carter!" Jamie wailed comically.

Spence growled ferociously and lunged for the child again. Jamie screeched and splashed, her laughter filling the air. Drawn by the interesting sounds, Sherman and Peabody came running through the open gate of the security fence that surrounded the pool. They bounced around the concrete pool skirting and yapped their excitement. Libby hadn't realized before how quiet her home had been. How much it had needed the laughter of a child to disturb the silence.

Her pensive thoughts scattered when a cold spray of water hit her squarely in the back of the head. She gasped, blinked, then looked in surprise at the pool. Jamie clung to the side with one hand, the other covering her mouth as she giggled at Libby's reaction. Spence lazily treaded water in the middle of the pool, his exaggeratedly innocent expression a dead giveaway to his guilt.

"Oops," he said when Libby's eyes met his. "Sorry about that."

She lifted an eyebrow. "It was an accident, I suppose."

"Of course."

"How would you like me to sic Sherman and Peabody on you?"

He glanced from her to the dogs lolling indolently at the side of the pool, contentedly watching the humans at play, then looked back at Libby. "I'm quivering in fear," he assured her gravely.

She chuckled at his ironic tone. Their gazes held.

"Aren't you coming in, Dr. Carter?" Jamie asked, innocently interrupting the suddenly taut moment.

Libby pulled her gaze from Spence's with an effort. "Sure," she said, hoping her smile looked more natural than it felt. She dropped her kimono over the back of a pool chair and walked down the steps into the pool, grateful for the coolness of the water. For some reason, the afternoon seemed to have suddenly grown several degrees warmer during the past few minutes.

AFTER HER SWIM, Libby climbed out of the pool and padded across the concrete to the covered bar conveniently attached to the back of the house. A small refrigerator was tucked under the bar, stocked with an assortment of canned drinks. "Anyone else want something to drink?" she asked Spence and Jamie, who were standing beside the pool, toweling off. "I've got colas, diet colas, fruit drinks, ginger ale or root beer."

Jamie chose root beer, Spence requested a cola. Libby pulled out a diet cola for herself and carried the drinks to one of the round wrought-iron tables beside the pool. She sat in one of the four chairs grouped around the table and started to towel dry her hair into a cap of damp curls. Spence opened his drink and took a chair across the table from Libby. Jamie drank a few sips of her root beer, then dashed across the yard with the dogs, who eagerly participated in a game of fetch the stick.

"Jamie's a delightful child," Libby said, smiling as she watched the trio at play. "So well behaved. She's a pleasure to have around."

"She's a good kid," Spence agreed and, while his expression didn't change, Libby thought she saw a gleam of pride light his dark eyes.

"You seem very close," she commented, trying not to sound as though she were prying.

He shrugged. "It's been just the two of us since she was five."

"You have no other family?"

Spence was looking away from Libby, watching Jamie playing with the dogs. For a moment, she thought he wasn't going to answer. Then he said, "My mother lives in Georgia with my stepfather and two half sisters."

"Do you see your family often?"

"No." He didn't elaborate.

Libby knew she shouldn't ask the next question, knew it was none of her business and suspected Spence wouldn't like it—but she couldn't resist. "Is, er, is Jamie's mother still living?"

She'd predicted correctly that Spence wouldn't like the question. His face closed up, turning hard and distant—much different from the smiling man who'd played water tag in the pool with his daughter such a short while earlier. "We're divorced," he said. "She has no interest now in me or Jamie."

"Oh. I'm—"

Spence stood abruptly. "I've got some things to do. Thanks for the use of the pool, Dr. Carter. Jamie enjoyed it."

He was gone before she could even tell him that he was welcome.

Obviously, Libby thought wryly, Jamie's mother was definitely off-limits as far as future conversations went.

It was just as obvious that Spence had been badly hurt by his ex-wife. That he was still hurting.

Libby's heart twisted. Maybe that explained in part why he'd seemed so oblivious to her as a woman. Maybe he was still in love with Jamie's mother. Would he have reacted that strongly to her question if he weren't still in love with her?

Michael Spencer was wrong for Libby in so many ways. She had to keep reminding herself of that.

If only he weren't the first man to really interest her in longer than she could even remember.

4

THE HAMMER RANG rhythmically against the nail as Spence attached new shingles to the barn roof where a leak had developed. A portable radio tuned to a country station sat on the ground beneath him, the music drifting quietly up to him. Alan Jackson's "Chattahoochee" was playing; Spence found himself pounding nails in time to the lively beat.

The afternoon sun was hot on his bare back. It felt good. Over the sound of the radio, he could hear Jamie talking to Mrs. Grandjean, who was sitting in the covered yard swing behind her house, rocking and sipping iced tea as she listened with apparent fascination to Jamie's babbling. It was Monday, and Libby had gone to her clinic. Spence was a bit surprised by how noticeable her absence was after her weekend at home.

It wasn't that he had any particular interest in her or anything, he assured himself. It was just that she'd stayed very visible during the two days she was home, watching him work the black horse, swimming with him and Jamie, working in her flower beds most of Sunday afternoon. Though there hadn't been any personal conversation between them since those few awkward minutes by the swimming pool, he'd been aware of her presence. She'd smiled brightly each time their glances had met as he'd gone about his maintenance chores, so he assumed he hadn't offended her with his abruptness after she'd asked about his ex-wife.

She really had a very nice smile.

He moved a few inches to his right and reached for another shingle. A drop of sweat trickled down his nose; he swiped at it with the back of his left hand. Alan Jackson's voice faded and a rollicking new tune by Sawyer Brown began. Spence whistled along between his teeth. Damn, that Mark Miller could belt one out, he thought with a music lover's appreciation of talent.

Just because country music had once torn his life apart didn't mean he couldn't enjoy it now, painful though the memories were at times.

He wondered if Libby liked music. He'd heard her humming as she'd weeded the flower beds, but he hadn't recognized the tune. Sounded like classical, of which he knew almost nothing. Libby seemed like the classy type to him, even when she'd been grubby and hot and dressed in cutoffs and a faded T-shirt as she'd worked in her gardens.

He remembered the way she'd looked in her black bathing suit. His first thought had been that she'd certainly been in good shape. Firm arms, high breasts, flat stomach, lean hips and long, muscular legs. He supposed in her line of work she'd have to be in good shape. He tried to picture her splattered with blood or dirt or the other hazards of her business. He could vaguely envision her that way—but even in that particular image, she still looked classy to him. Poised and calm and confident.

He suddenly realized that he'd been sitting in the same position for several long moments, thinking about

Libby Carter. He shook his head in wry self-derision and fitted another nail to a corner of the shingle.

The hammer slammed against his thumb when a familiar silky voice drifted up from the radio to glide seductively into his ears.

Spence dropped the hammer, cursed viciously and lifted the throbbing thumb to his mouth. *Damn*, that hurt. When was the last time he'd stupidly smashed his thumb with a hammer?

The woman on the radio began the second verse of the sentimental ballad. Spence's scowl deepened. He could remember a time when that same voice had crooned that same song solely for him.

He was assaulted by memories of glittering copper hair and brilliant blue eyes, of a lushly curved body and a willing, hungry mouth. He remembered being young and in love and happy. And then he remembered the tearing pain that had followed when his wife had left him and their daughter so she could pursue her own dreams. Had she ever looked back? Had she ever thought of everything she'd given up and wondered if it had been worth all she'd gained? And underneath those old, oft-repeated questions was the one that still bothered him most—*had it been his fault that she'd left him?* Had there been anything he could have done to make her stay?

From her place on the swing beside Mrs. Grandjean, Jamie laughed. He glanced her way, and thought of her tenth birthday a few months back, which had passed without a gift, a call or even a card from her mother. Jamie had tried to hide her disappointment, though she hadn't been entirely successful. Spence, of course, had been furious—and had suffered the rejection as deeply as his child, along with a healthy load of guilt that he and Delilah had done this to Jamie. But Jamie had refused to talk about it, and Spence hadn't pushed her. He didn't much like talking about his ex-wife, either.

Spence mentally tuned out the radio and turned with a determined frown to the task he'd begun. He had the roof to finish, and then a clogged downspout on the house to clean out. After that, he planned to work with Tennessee for an hour or so.

He didn't have time to sit around thinking about women—his ex-wife *or* his shapely employer.

"HOW'S YOUR NEW caretaker working out?" Libby's partner, Paul Baker, asked during a rare break from work on Tuesday afternoon. He'd appeared in the doorway of her office and offered her an apple, which she'd politely refused. Now he stood leaning idly against the door frame, polishing the apple against his shirt as he watched her.

Libby glanced up from the canine geriatric workup she'd been studying. She'd been deliberately trying *not* to think of Spence, which wasn't as hard to do at work where she stayed too busy, but Paul's question brought Spence's lean, hard face vividly to her mind. "He's, er, working out just fine."

"His kid causing any problems?" Married less than a year, Paul still hadn't decided that he wanted children. He loved animals, but human children, he'd often said, were a species he simply couldn't understand.

"Jamie's no trouble at all," Libby said firmly. "She's an adorable child. I'm sure she misbehaves at times like any normal child, but I haven't seen it yet."

Paul bit into the apple, crunching noisily. Just as Libby had tuned him out and started concentrating on the medical report again, he said, "Sounds to me like you're smitten."

Libby felt her cheeks warm. "Don't be ridiculous. I hardly know the guy."

Paul's eyebrows rose slowly. "I was talking about the kid."

"Oh."

"So tell me a little more about the kid's father."

She swallowed a sigh, still silently cursing her verbal slip. Paul was like a dog with a juicy bone when he stumbled onto something intriguing; he'd never stop asking questions until she'd satisfied his curiosity. "Spence is okay. He's a good father, a hard worker and seems to have a special talent for working with horses. He's training Tennessee. If he does as good a job as I think he will, I'm planning to recommend him to some horse owners who've been looking for trainers."

"And how old did you say the guy is?"

"Somewhere in his early thirties."

"Just the right age."

"For horse training?" Libby asked sarcastically.

Paul grinned. "For you, toots."

"God, I hate it when you call me that."

"Oh, sorry. I always forget." But he wasn't sorry, and he didn't forget. Libby shook her head, knowing the truth was visible in his mischievous green eyes.

"Go away, Paul. I have work to do."

As though in confirmation, Debbie Smith, their receptionist, appeared behind Paul in the doorway with a stack of pink slips of paper clutched in her hand. "Dr. Carter? You've got several calls to return," she said. "And Dr. Baker, Mrs. Kelsey is here with Gus. He's, um, eating the couch in the waiting area at the moment."

Paul groaned and rolled his eyes. "When is that woman ever going to start training that animal? Okay, Deb, send her back. And tell Jeff I may need him to give me a hand. Gus isn't real fond of being poked and prodded."

Debbie's grin was bright against her coffee-colored skin. "Yes, Dr. Baker," she said, obviously amused by his exaggerated dread of his next patient. "Jeff's probably hiding behind the X-ray screen again. I think he's been there ever since Mrs. Kelsey dragged Gus in."

Libby was relieved when she was alone again. Even returning phone calls was preferable to being grilled about Spence by her unashamedly nosy partner. She wasn't ready to talk about feelings she hadn't even examined too closely herself.

She took a deep breath and dialed the first number on the stack. "Mrs. Kennedy?" she said a moment later. "It's Dr. Carter. Fluffy isn't feeling well today?"

ON THURSDAY, Libby returned home a little earlier than usual from the clinic, having had a blessedly light day at work. She'd needed the break—it had been a rough week so far, and next week would be worse, since Paul would be taking his wife for a much-needed trip to the mountains. Libby knew her partner deserved the time off, but she wasn't looking forward to being on twenty-four-hour call for an entire week, even though another local vet had promised to be available to help out if needed. Paul had assured her that he would make it up to her by giving her a week off soon. Libby had agreed, but had no plans for a vacation just now. There was always so much to be done....

The sounds of children's squeals and laughter caught her attention as soon as she climbed out of her functional Explorer. She heard water splashing and headed for the pool to investigate. Her dogs met her at the end of the driveway, welcoming her with noisy enthusiasm, then fell in behind her as she walked around the corner of the house. The sheer pleasure in the voices drifting her way made her smile in response. It really was nice to hear children's laughter around the place, she thought a bit wistfully.

She found her grandmother sitting with a neighbor beside the pool, sipping iced tea, chatting and watching the three children cavorting in the water. Libby leaned over to kiss her grandmother's cheek. "Hi, Gran." And then she turned to their guest. "Hi, Sophie. How nice to see you."

A few years older than Libby, Sophie Patterson lived in the next house down the road. She smiled a greeting. "Libby, it's been a coon's age since I saw you last," she teased. "Where've you been keeping yourself?"

"At the clinic, mostly," Libby admitted. She pulled a soft drink out of the bar refrigerator, then joined her grandmother and neighbor at the wrought-iron table.

"Hi, Dr. Carter!" Jamie called from the pool, her wet copper hair streaming down her back, her water-beaded face flushed with exertion. "Patty and Leo came to swim with me this afternoon."

"So I see." Libby looked back at Sophie. "Patty will be in fifth grade this year, won't she?"

"Yes. She and Jamie will go to the same school. Emma and I thought it would make Jamie more comfortable if she knows at least one child when school starts next week. And you know how Patty loves making new friends."

Libby watched eight-year-old Leo barrel off the end of the diving board in an obvious effort to impress the girls. She smiled. "Leo's really growing. He'll be in, what, third grade?"

"Yeah. Look at the way he's flirting with Jamie. Leo always has had a thing for older women."

The women laughed and then Gran changed the subject, catching Libby up on the latest neighborhood gossip that she and Sophie had been discussing before Libby's arrival.

After a while, Libby glanced casually around the place and asked in what she hoped what a lightly nonchalant tone, "So where's Spence this afternoon?"

"Oh, he's cutting hay for Mr. Whittaker," Gran explained. "He'll be going back tomorrow afternoon and probably most of the day Saturday to finish up. He's been getting up early the past couple of days to get his chores done around here before he leaves for Whittaker's place. Jamie's been staying with me."

Libby lifted an eyebrow. "You didn't mention that before."

"You've been busy, dear," Gran remarked. "Leaving early, coming home late. We've hardly had time to talk."

"I know," Libby admitted, pushing a hand through her curls. "It has been a rough week, and next week's going to be worse."

Sophie and Gran both shook their heads. "You work too hard, Libby," Gran said, as she had many times before.

"Much too hard," Sophie agreed. "You're not getting any younger, Libby. You need to be finding a husband, having a few kids of your own. Why, when I was your age, I already had both mine."

"Libby's had plenty of opportunities to get married," Gran defended her loyally. "She's just waiting for the right man, aren't you, dear?"

"Gran, you make it sound as though I've turned down dozens of proposals. There was only one," Libby said indulgently.

"Hal MacNulty," Gran said with a shudder. "What you ever saw in that man . . ."

"Hal was nice," Libby said without taking offense. "I just wasn't in love with him."

"Nice." Gran gave what might have been a snort in someone less dignified. "He was a life-insurance salesman. I think that sums it up well enough."

Libby shook her head in resignation. They'd had this conversation several times and she had yet to understand her grandmother's antipathy toward insurance salesmen. "Never mind," she said, aware that Sophie was watching with a grin. "My social life will take care of itself, thank you."

"Not without a little help from you, it won't," Sophie retorted. "Can't expect the right man to come ringing your doorbell, Libby. Sometimes you just have to go out looking for him."

Libby, of course, couldn't help thinking of the man who *had* recently appeared at her door. She pretended to be distracted by the antics of the children, not wanting either of the women to notice her sudden preoccupation.

What was this *obsession* she was developing toward her new caretaker? she asked herself in exasperation. Okay, so the guy was attractive. Well, sexy as all get out, to be honest. But he paid her no more attention that he did her horses—not as much, actually. It was foolish of her to waste so much concentration on a man who'd made it clear enough that he didn't return that interest.

SPENCE ALL BUT DRAGGED himself home just before dark on Saturday. He was filthy, tired, aching. His bum leg felt as though he'd put it through a wringer a few times, which proved it hadn't healed as well as he'd hoped. How was he going to get back into rodeo if he couldn't even drive a tractor for a few days without feeling as though he'd been beaten?

Damn, but he felt old.

The cottage lights were on, shining in welcome through the plain cotton curtains. He pictured Jamie inside waiting for him and tried to smile. His cheek muscles were too weary to respond. He couldn't imagine what his life would be like without his kid to come home to. Wouldn't be worth living, as far as he was concerned.

He reached out and tried the doorknob, nodding in satisfaction to find it locked. Good. Jamie was following his instructions, keeping the doors locked when he wasn't there. He pushed his key into the lock and turned the knob.

Jamie was sitting curled up on the couch—but she wasn't alone. Libby Carter sat beside her, and their heads were bent over the book from which Libby read aloud while Jamie listened in fascination. They were so absorbed they hadn't even heard Spence come in.

He watched for a long moment with a funny feeling somewhere deep inside him. Jamie looked so content snuggled against Libby's side. And Libby's voice was so gentle and soothing and nurturing that Spence was damned tempted to curl up beside her himself.

As though she'd suddenly sensed him standing there, Libby looked up. Her eyes widened. "Oh. We—I didn't hear you come in."

"Obviously." She looked cool and clean and fresh in her white shirt and white jeans. He felt filthy in comparison, acutely aware of the dirt and hay crusting his hair and clothes. "I, uh, need a shower."

"You look tired, Dad," Jamie said sympathetically.

"I am," he admitted.

"Dr. Carter was just staying with me till you got home. She brought dinner. Gran made it for us, 'cause she knew you'd be too tired to cook after a long day in the hay fields."

Spence's smile felt forced. "That was nice of her."

Libby closed her book and stood. "We'll read the rest of the story another time, Jamie. I'm sure your father would like to clean up and relax now."

Spence felt compelled to say something. "Uh, thanks for keeping an eye out for her. Hope you didn't have anything else to do tonight."

"No, I had no plans. I needed a peaceful night myself," she answered with a smile.

He wondered why an attractive single woman like Libby was home with nothing to do on a Saturday night. Didn't she date? If not, how come? She was certainly pleasant enough company. He'd ask her out himself, if he hadn't vowed long ago to confine himself to the occasional women who wanted nothing more from him than a little fun and a single night's pleasure.

He had no doubt that Libby was not of the one-night-stand persuasion. She was home-and-hearth-and-honey-I'm-home if he'd ever seen the type. That is, if she'd ever drag herself away from that job of hers long enough to find herself a man. And wouldn't she just love it if he expressed *that* thought aloud?

"Your dinner's in the oven, wrapped in foil," Libby said, pausing to stand beside him for a moment on her way to the door. "It should still be warm enough, but if not you could always pop it in the microwave for a couple of minutes."

"I'll take care of it."

"I'm sure you will." Her tone was dry.

"Tell your grandmother thanks for me, okay?"

"I will. Good night, Spence."

He realized it was the first time she'd actually called him by name. "Good night, Dr. Carter."

She gave him a chiding look. "Libby," she corrected him. "I'm not your doctor."

He nodded, but didn't repeat her first name. "Good night."

He thought he saw her shaking her head as she walked out and closed the front door behind her.

SPENCE CRAWLED into bed a couple of hours later, so tired he groaned when he pulled the sheet up to his chin. He fell asleep immediately, but his sleep was restless, disturbed by bizarre dreams.

He dreamed of Libby at one point. She was dressed all in white, and she was reading to Jamie. They looked so content, so right together, that he felt left out. He hovered on the sidelines of the dream, torn between a wistful longing to join them and a dull anger that someone was taking his child away from him.

And then she looked up at him and her eyes were brilliant blue, not green as they should have been. "Say my name," she said, and it wasn't Libby's voice, but another woman's—a voice that would be instantly recognized by half of America.

Her short blond curls seemed to lengthen, darken, until they blazed like living fire around her smooth, bare shoulders. "Say my name, Michael," she crooned, reaching out for him with soft hands tipped with long, dark-red nails.

Jamie had disappeared, leaving him alone with the woman. She glided closer to him. "Say my name," she whispered in the voice that had never failed to clench his chest into a tight ache of desire.

"Delilah," he croaked, and reached out for her.

She laughed and skillfully evaded his grasp. She turned, and flashed a dazzling smile to the starry-eyed audience who had suddenly appeared to surround them. "I love you!" she called, and she wasn't talking to Spence. "I love you all."

And she disappeared into the adoring crowd. Spence was left alone—again.

He woke with a start, his fists clenched, his forehead dampened with perspiration, the sounds of cheering fans still ringing in his ears.

He rolled onto his stomach and buried his face in the pillow. One fist slammed against the mattress. "Shit," he growled, furious with himself for letting his past rule his dreams. So damned tired of the pain.

It was always Jamie's sweet face he brought to mind when he needed calming. He pictured her now, her trusting blue eyes, her contagious smile. Oddly enough, he was seeing her again as he had when he'd returned home that evening, curled on the sofa at Libby's side, basking in the warmth and affection the woman offered. And it was Libby's voice he remembered now, reading to his daughter in that gentle, soothing tone.

He finally slept again, without dreaming this time. When he woke early the next morning, he crawled immediately out of the bed and busied himself with chores, refusing to think about his dreams. Any part of them.

5

LIBBY WAS DRESSED and ready for work at the usual time on Monday. But instead of climbing into her Explorer and being on her way, she found herself lingering at the end of the long driveway with Gran, Spence and Jamie as they awaited the bright yellow bus that would take Jamie for her first day of school.

"You're sure you have your lunch money?" Spence asked for the third time.

Jamie patted the outside zippered pocket on her bright pink backpack. "I've got it, Dad."

"Don't forget your bus number this afternoon," Gran fretted, leaning over the front of her walker to smooth Jamie's neatly brushed copper hair, free of the baseball cap for a change.

"I won't forget, Gran," Jamie promised.

Libby thought the child looked adorable in the new purple jeans and colorful striped top Spence had bought her for school. Jamie had eagerly told her all about the four new outfits her father had purchased for her at the same discount store where he'd bought her school supplies from the list he'd been provided when he'd registered Jamie at the school. Jamie even had new sneakers, which were so white they were almost blinding—a pristine condition that Libby knew wouldn't last long.

"I hope you have a wonderful first day at school, Jamie," she said.

Jamie spoke confidently enough, though a trace of nervousness was visible in her eyes. "It'll be okay," she assured the three hovering adults. "I liked my teacher when I met her yesterday afternoon at the welcome-back-to-school reception. And Patty's in Mrs. Bennett's class, too, so I'll have one friend at least."

"You'll have a dozen by the end of the day," Gran predicted.

"You behave yourself, you hear?" Spence bade his daughter. "No talking in class. Pay attention to the schoolwork. And try to sit still in your seat. No squirming around."

Jamie shifted her weight restlessly from one foot to the other, already squirming. But she promised, anyway. "Okay, Dad. I'll be good."

His face suddenly softened with a smile. "Yeah," he said gruffly and tugged her against him for a quick hug. "I know you will."

Libby swallowed the lump in her throat. "I think I see the bus coming," she said.

"Yeah, that's it," Jamie agreed, peering down the road. She hugged her father again. "'Bye, Dad. I'll help you with the chores when I get home, okay?"

"Okay, punkin. I'll save some of them for you."

Jamie reached up to kiss Gran's cheek. "'Bye, Gran."

"'Bye, sweetie. I'll have some fresh-baked cookies waiting when you come home."

Jamie grinned her approval. "All right!"

And then she turned to Libby. "'Bye," she said, her smile a bit shy now as she looked up at Libby.

Libby couldn't resist leaning over to brush her lips against the child's soft cheek. "'Bye, Jamie. Have fun."

The bus pulled to a stop, red lights flashing, children chattering noisily inside. Jamie gave them one last, brave smile and climbed onto the steps, clutching her backpack and suddenly looking very small and vulnerable. The driver, a heavyset, amazingly cheerful-looking woman, waved at them and took off in a cloud of dust.

The lump was back in Libby's throat, and it seemed to have grown. She sneaked a peek at Spence from beneath her lashes. His face could have been carved from hardwood. Catching her gaze, he settled his black hat onto his head and turned his back to the road. "I've got work to do," he drawled. "You need any help getting back to the house, Mrs. Grandjean?"

Gran shook her gray head at him, her expression stern. "I'm perfectly capable of walking to the house. Run along with you."

He flashed her a quick smile. "Yes, ma'am. I'll be working on that loose siding at the back of the house if you need me." He glanced at Libby. "You're running late to work, aren't you?"

"Yes," she admitted. "And I'd better be going. Paul's out of town this week, so it's going to be a madhouse." She kissed her grandmother. "I'll probably be late."

"I know. Try not to work too hard."

"I'll try," Libby answered, but knew it was a promise she wouldn't be able to keep.

BY LATE SATURDAY afternoon, Libby felt as though she'd been run over by Jamie's school bus. She'd known the load would be heavy while Paul was away, but she'd had no way of knowing how bad it really would turn out to be. Even with the occasional assistance of a couple of veterinarian friends, the work was almost more than she could handle.

In addition to her regular work load, there seemed to be a spate of animal emergencies that kept her running. Jeff, the young man who worked for her summers, weekends and after school, injured his arm in a motorcycle accident and had to take several days off. She found another teenager to take his place, but the substitute needed training that she had little time to offer. And it didn't help anything when the clinic's main computer crashed late in the week, keeping the billing records inaccessible until a repairman arrived to set things straight.

By the end of the week, Libby had been scratched, bruised and bitten, and had been splattered with blood, vomit and urine. Those, of course, were the job hazards she expected and usually took in stride. It was all the other stuff that made her crazy.

She arrived home at about dinnertime Saturday evening—the earliest she'd been home all week. Telling her concerned grandmother she wasn't hungry, she changed into a clean T-shirt, jeans and scuffed western boots and headed for the barn. She visited Tennessee for a few minutes, then saddled Alabama and swung herself onto the mare's back. She really needed a quiet ride in the woods, she thought with a long sigh. She had a good three hours left until dark, and she planned to use them all.

She dismounted to open the back gate out of her pasture, led the horse through it, then locked the gate and remounted. Alabama danced a little, and Libby patted the animal's glossy neck. It had been too long since they'd had this chance, she thought with a sigh. Bama seemed to have missed their long rides as much as Libby had.

She gave the horse its head, her face turned eagerly toward the wooded hills waiting for them across a wide clearing.

AN HOUR LATER, Libby sat comfortably in the saddle while Alabama munched lazily on a patch of tall grass. They had reached one of Libby's favorite places, a clearing at the top of one of the higher hills in the area. She could see a long way from here—farmland, mostly. Rolling green hills, an occasional patch of trees, a few narrow winding roads, a glimmer of water at the horizon. The Arkansas River. She knew that if the trees behind her suddenly vanished, she'd be able to see the modern Little Rock skyline. She preferred this view, this illusion that the busy, noisy, bustling life of the city was far away.

She took a deep breath, letting the clean, crisp air clear away some of the lingering tension of the work-week. Birds sang in the trees and a squirrel chattered from a branch somewhere above her head. Far in the distance, she thought she heard the muted roar of a tractor.

She frowned in response to the new sounds suddenly coming from the trail behind her. Sounded like another horse, she thought, turning in the saddle to look. She knew a couple of other local horse owners who occasionally rode this trail, but she rarely encountered anyone during her rides. Who—?

Her eyes widened when she recognized the rider . . . and the horse. "Spence!" she said, at the same time Alabama snorted a greeting to Tennessee. "What are you doing here?"

"Your grandmother said you were out here somewhere," he answered, pushing his hat back with his thumb so that she could better see his face. "I thought I'd follow you and give Ten a workout. Unless you want to be alone?"

"No," she assured him. She looked at the black horse beneath him, who was tasting the tall grass Alabama had found so appetizing. "You've worked wonders with him. He looks perfectly content to have you riding him."

"He's a good horse," Spence said off handedly. "Fast learner. Uh, think you'd ever consider selling him?"

Libby blinked in surprise. "Selling him?" she repeated. "To you?"

He nodded. "To me."

"You want to train him for rodeo?"

"Yeah. He's got a lot of potential. Reminds me of Red Devil."

"Red Devil?"

"My last horse. I had to have him put down after the car accident that busted my leg."

Spence's eyes had darkened and Libby heard the trace of regret in his voice. He'd obviously been attached to his horse. She knew he loved the animals and treated them well. But sell Tennessee? She hadn't even considered the idea before.

"I'll think about it," she told him. "I bought him to keep Bama company, but I've grown fond of him. I'm not sure I want to sell him."

Spence shrugged. "No rush. I can't pay for him until my insurance settlement comes through, anyway."

"Insurance settlement?" She spoke without thinking, then winced as she realized that she had been parroting him like an idiot. Why did this man turn her into such a babbling wreck when she usually managed to carry on a coherent, reasonably intelligent conversation with other men?

"From the car accident," he explained.

"Oh." She brushed a hand through her breeze-tossed curls. "Was Jamie with you in the accident?"

"Yeah. She wasn't hurt, thank God."

Tennessee shifted restlessly beneath Spence. "Were you planning to ride any farther?" Spence asked, controlling the horse with a tighter rein and a few soothing words.

"Yes. The trail winds around to the other side of the hill. Would you like to ride with me?" she asked, feeling like an infatuated schoolgirl.

"Guess so. Your grandmother's teaching Jamie to knit, so I'm free for another hour or so before dinner."

Libby smiled, thinking of her own knitting lessons when she was Jamie's age. She hadn't shown much natural aptitude for the craft. Maybe Jamie would be better at it. "Gran's very fond of Jamie," she said.

Spence nodded as he guided Tennessee. "The feeling's mutual. Jamie's fond of your grandmother. I, uh, guess she likes having a couple of women to talk to for a change."

"You've done a wonderful job with her, Spence. It couldn't have been easy for a man alone to raise a little girl."

He shrugged again. "We get by. But I think it's going to get harder as she gets older. There are some things I guess only a woman would know to tell her."

Libby smiled. "Like warning her that white hose make the legs look thicker? Or that bright colored eye shadows dull the natural color of the eye? Or that overbleaching can make a woman's hair look like a pile of old barn straw?"

Spence chuckled. "Yeah. That sort of thing." He slanted her a sideways glance from beneath the shadow of his hat. "Do white hose really make your legs look thicker?"

"They add a good five pounds per leg. No one but nurses should ever wear them," Libby assured him gravely.

"Gotta admit that's a new one for me."

"And don't forget the other things she'll have to learn. Like never wearing white shoes before Easter or after Labor Day in the South. Or never having pins in her underwear in case there's an accident and she has to go to the hospital."

"I knew about that underwear thing," he said. "My mother used to remind me not to have any holes in mine for the same reason. I never could quite figure out why the doctors would care what shape your underwear's in if you're hurt bad enough to go to the hospital."

"And then there's PMS," Libby said teasingly.

Spence groaned. "Yeah. I know about that one, too. My ex-wife —" He stopped abruptly, as though appalled that he'd spoken about a subject that was taboo. "Uh, watch that low branch ahead," he said instead, pointing to a branch that Libby would have had to go out of her way to brush up against.

She wanted so badly to ask more about his ex-wife. Why had she and Spence broken up? Why didn't Jamie ever mention her mother? Didn't the woman want to see the beautiful daughter Spence was raising alone? Had he given her any choice in that matter, or was she truly as uninterested as Spence had claimed her to be?

But Libby firmly pushed those questions and any related ones to the back of her mind. Spence had talked to her more during the past half hour than he had in the weeks he'd been working for her. She didn't want to alienate him now with her unwelcome curiosity.

"My mother died when I was not much older than Jamie," she said instead, pretending she hadn't noticed his aborted comment. "Gran taught me most of what I've learned about being a woman—particularly a Southern woman," she added with a slight smile.

"Your grandmother's a real lady."

Her smile deepened at his unconscious imitation of her thoughts. "Yes. She is."

"Your father still alive?"

It was one of the few personal questions he'd ever asked her. "No. He died three years ago. I bought my house and land with the inheritance he left."

"So it's just you and your grandmother now?"

"I have a few aunts, uncles and cousins scattered around the state. We have an official family reunion every other year and see each other occasionally in between. But most of the time, yes, it's just Gran and me."

"Seems to be working out."

"We get by," she said, deliberately mocking his drawl.

He gave her what might have been a quick grin and clucked Tennessee on when the horse hesitated at a rough patch of ground.

SPENCE HELD TENNESSEE back and let Libby ride slightly ahead of him when the path narrowed. He couldn't help noticing that the view from the back wasn't at all bad. She looked good on a horse. Back straight, hips slim, thighs gripping the horse in a way that couldn't help but make a man start thinking of . . .

He cleared his throat. Tennessee shied, and Spence soothed him, silently chiding himself for letting his hormones get the best of him. Okay, so it had been a while since he'd gone to bed with a woman. A long while, to be bluntly honest. And Libby Carter was certainly attractive enough, if one cared for the wholesome, fresh-faced, small-town-values type. But he would keep his distance. All that talk about Jamie needing a woman around—well, that was just the sort of thinking he didn't want to encourage. He had no intention of settling down in one place any time soon and he damned sure didn't intend to get married again. Not for Jamie, or any other reason.

A man should only have to visit hell once in his lifetime.

Libby looked over her shoulder and smiled. "You're awfully quiet all of a sudden."

He shifted his weight in the saddle and nodded. "Just enjoying the ride."

"It is nice up here, isn't it?"

"Yeah. I can see why you like it so much."

"What do you do in the rodeo, Spence? I'm not very familiar with the sport, I'm afraid. When I think rodeo, I think of bucking broncos or wild bulls."

"I've ridden some rough stock in my time," he admitted, "but I prefer roping."

"Team roping?" she asked, obviously reciting a term she'd heard somewhere.

He shook his head. "I work alone."

"Now why doesn't that surprise me?" she muttered, then lifted an innocent eyebrow at him when he frowned at her. "I've heard of something called bull-dogging. What is that, and do you ever do it?"

He couldn't help smiling. "Basically it's jumping off your horse and wrestling a steer to the ground. And, yeah, I've done some of it. I still prefer roping."

"Are you any good?"

He grimaced and held up his right hand, tilting it from side to side to indicate that he was somewhere between great and average. "I'd be better if I didn't have a little problem with accidents," he added, rather surprised that he'd made the admission to her. It wasn't a topic he usually discussed, even when his rodeo friends ragged him about it.

"What little problem?" Libby asked curiously, still half-turned in her saddle so that she could look at him as they talked.

"Look where you're going," he advised curtly, watching her swiftly catch her balance when Alabama stumbled over a loose rock.

She turned obligingly to watch the path ahead, but persisted. "What little problem with accidents?"

"I seem to attract them. A buddy calls me an accident magnet. Thinks it's a hell of a joke that I've somehow managed to break two-thirds of the bones in my body. Every time I get on a winning streak on the circuit, I end up breaking something and putting myself out of commission again. Even earned myself a nickname—'Splint' Spencer."

He'd thought to amuse her with that confession, and knew he'd simply wanted to see her nice smile again.

Libby didn't smile. "You hurt yourself that often?"

He was self-conscious now. He shrugged. "Not really," he lied. "It's just a joke among the other guys."

"What will happen to Jamie if you manage to break your neck next time you jump off a horse and wrestle a steer to the ground?"

He stiffened at the question, even as he recognized the quick flash of regret in Libby's expression. She had spoken without thinking, he supposed, but that didn't make the question any easier to hear. Especially when it was one that had occurred to him during more than a few long, sleepless nights.

"I'm not going to break my neck," he growled. "And I'm taking care of my kid."

Yeah, right, Spencer. Taking damned good care of her. Look at all you've done for her so far.

He ignored the nagging voice that mocked him in his head. He'd been avoiding that tenacious voice a lot lately.

"I'm sorry," Libby said quietly. "I shouldn't have said that. I didn't mean it the way it sounded."

Yes, she had, but he didn't bother to argue with her. Instead, he pointed out the deer ahead that had been startled into leaping right across their path. Libby cooperated with the change of subject again. He only wished her question was as easily forgotten as it had been evaded.

IT WAS GETTING DARK by the time they returned from their ride. Spence opened the gate to the pasture and closed it behind Libby when she rode through, leading Tennessee. He remounted, then looked at the expanse of level pasture lying between them and the barn. "Wonder if Tennessee's ready for a gallop," he said.

Libby grinned. "Let's find out." She touched her heels to Alabama's sides and made a quick, clucking sound. "Go for it, Bama!"

Spence wasted a few good seconds admiring the way Libby looked, bent over the neck of her racing horse.

Tennessee handled the run well enough, considering his inexperience. They reached the barn after Libby, but Spence didn't mind since he hadn't been competing.

Libby and Spence worked side by side unsaddling the horses and brushing them down. Libby fed them while Spence stowed the riding gear in the tack room.

It had been kind of nice riding together, Spence mused, inhaling the familiar smells of horse, hay and feed. Delilah had never liked riding. Got her all sweaty and smelly, she'd complained.

And, damn it, he was thinking about her again!

He suddenly noticed that Libby was struggling to empty a newly opened, fifty-pound bag of grain into the feed bin. He moved forward swiftly to take it from her. "I'll get that."

"I can do it," she insisted proudly, not immediately releasing the bag.

They stood hip to hip, hands overlapping on the feed bag, faces only inches apart. Spence froze. He noticed for the first time that there were little flecks of gold in Libby's green eyes, and that she had exactly five freckles across the bridge of her nose. And he noticed for maybe the hundredth time that she had a very nice mouth.

He wondered if it tasted as sweet as it looked.

Libby's eyes widened, as though she'd read the question in his eyes. Her lips parted, and the tip of her tongue darted out to moisten them in a nervous gesture that he thought was involuntary, but was damned sexy all the same. He felt her breath on his cheek as he lowered his head, and he saw the way her breasts lifted when she drew a quick breath.

"Libby?"

Jamie's voice came from the barn doorway. Spence and Libby sprang apart as suddenly and as guiltily as though they'd been caught doing something indecent.

"What—what is it, Jamie?" Libby asked, and Spence noticed that her voice seemed half an octave higher than usual.

"Gran sent me out to get you. She said to tell you Mrs. Dunlap called and said her poodle is having trouble breathing. Mrs. Dunlap wants to know if you can come take care of it."

Libby pushed a hand through her hair. Spence wondered if he only imagined that it wasn't quite steady. He shoved his own into the pockets of his jeans.

"Would you mind running back to the house and telling Gran to call Mrs. Dunlap and let her know I'm on my way?" Libby asked Jamie, and suddenly she was all business, her movements brisk and efficient, her voice calm. "Tell her I'll be home later. I don't need to go in. My emergency bag is in my Explorer."

Jamie nodded, her eyes round. "I'll tell her."

"Thank you, Jamie." Libby headed for the doorway in the child's wake.

"Libby?" Spence was aware it was the first time he'd called her by name.

She looked over her shoulder, her expression faintly startled. Maybe she'd noticed it, too. "Yes?"

"You need any help or anything? I could come along if—"

"Thank you for offering, Spence, but I'll be fine. This is just part of my job."

He nodded and stepped back, knowing he'd just been politely dismissed. And he wondered why he found himself resenting that she'd dismissed him quite so easily, especially after—

After what, Spencer? he asked himself impatiently. *Nothing happened. Nothing is going to happen, if you use your head for something other than a hat rack. Get a grip, will you?*

Suddenly realizing that he was standing in the barn alone while the two horses munched on their dinner, he muttered a curse and headed for the cottage. He was hungry, too. Time to fix something for himself and Jamie.

He wondered if Libby would have a chance to eat dinner that evening. And then he wondered why it bothered him so badly that she might not.

6

DURING THE NEXT few weeks, they all settled into a
routine of sorts. Libby left for work each morning at
about the same time Jamie's school bus arrived. Gran
was finally able to abandon the walker, which made it
easier for her to take care of the household chores she
claimed for her own—cooking, baking, light house-
work, laundry. She spent her afternoons with Jamie,
who sought her out for lovingly homemade after-
school snacks, then worked on homework and needle-
work projects in Gran's cozy kitchen until it was time
to rejoin her father in their cottage.

In the mornings, Spence handled repairs and routine maintenance, yard and garden work and took care
of the barn and animals. Every day at noon, he left for
the part-time job Libby had discovered for him on a
large quarter-horse ranch some ten miles west of Libby's place. He returned home at six to prepare dinner
for his daughter, after which they took care of their own
household chores and then often crashed in front of the
TV for a couple of hours of what Spence considered to
be quality time with his kid before her bedtime. Some
evenings they played the board games Jamie loved, or
listened to music and talked about her day at school.
On weekends, Jamie trailed after Spence as he did his

chores around the place, and then the two of them often went out for burgers or pizza or a movie.

It wasn't a bad life, Spence had to concede sometime during the middle of October. He hadn't even gotten particularly bored with it. Yet.

He still hadn't received the insurance settlement, though the lawyer in Colorado kept promising that it would all be taken care of soon. He was glad he'd found this job, which provided a safe environment for Jamie—probably the most stable routine she'd ever known. She was making all As at school, and was a model student, her teacher had assured him after he'd suffered through a long, boring PTA meeting one evening last week. She was making friends among her schoolmates. She loved the dogs, the horses, Gran and Libby. She was healthy and happy and content. And Spence was beginning to worry that she wasn't going to want to leave here when it was time to move on.

Jamie's emotional attachment to Gran and Libby concerned him most. He thought about it as he mucked out Alabama's stall late one evening. Libby stayed so busy with her work that none of them saw her all that much, though Jamie was very fond of her. During the few hours that she did spend at home, Libby often went out of her way to visit awhile with Jamie, though she seemed to have been making a practice of avoiding any more one-on-one encounters with Spence after their ride through the woods together.

He wondered if she remembered, as he did, that awkward moment when they'd stood so close, his mouth inches from hers, their gazes locked in sudden, sensual awareness.

Pushing that uncomfortable memory to the back of his mind, he thought again of Jamie's growing attachment to Libby's grandmother. Spence's mother had never been much of a grandmother to Jamie, having been busy tending her own twin daughters, Linda and Tina, born to her and her second husband, Carl Holiday, long after she'd stopped expecting any more children. The twins were only seniors in high school now; their mother still a couple of years short of sixty. Had Jamie missed having a traditional, silver-haired, cookie-baking grandmother, like Libby's "Gran"?

Had Jamie also missed having a real home? Had she felt deprived by growing up in a battered RV with no one but her life-scarred father to call family? Would she resent him for pulling her back into that nomadic life again?

But what else did he have to offer her? It was the only life he'd known for so long that he wasn't sure he could make it any other way, despite the fairly comfortable routines he'd fallen into here in Little Rock. He couldn't go on indefinitely doing odd jobs and part-time work. The insurance settlement wouldn't be enough to set them up with a place of their own, or anything like that. Mostly it would just let him buy a new horse and maybe replace some of the rodeo purses he might have won had he not been incapacitated for these months.

Okay, so he couldn't rodeo forever. As Mrs. Grandjean had so bluntly pointed out, that career was necessarily curtailed by the passage of years. And Spence wasn't getting any younger.

For the past few years, he'd had an almost pathological aversion to thinking about the future, a strange inability to plan beyond a few weeks ahead. It hadn't always been that way. He'd once had dreams for the future—himself and Delilah on a nice little ranch somewhere with Jamie and maybe a couple other kids. But that had been before Delilah had shattered those plans with her own dreams of fame and fortune. And rather than giving up his dreams to help her pursue hers, he'd forced her to make a choice.

She hadn't chosen him.

"Spence?"

Libby's voice drew him out of his grim thoughts. He rested the tines of the pitchfork on the ground and leaned against the stick. "In here."

She came through the barn door. She was wearing a pale blue shirt with the sleeves rolled up, a pair of close-fitting jeans and laced-up boots and looked completely at home in the musty, shadowy, artificially-lit barn. She smiled when she saw him, and though her smile was as friendly as ever, he thought he detected a trace of self-consciousness in her eyes. "Hi," she said.

"Hi. What's up?"

"I wanted to ask your opinion about something."

He leaned more comfortably against the pitchfork. "Okay."

She rested an elbow against a stall door, propping one foot on the lower rung of the railing. "Someone brought an injured kitten to the clinic a few days ago. It was in bad shape—sick, hurt, half-starved. I wasn't even sure it would make it, but it did, and now it seems to be thriving. Pretty little thing. Gray, with four white stockings. Male."

Spence wasn't at all sure where this conversation was headed. "What about it?"

"I thought—if it's okay with you, of course—that I'd ask Jamie if she wants it."

Spence was caught off guard. "A pet? I don't know—"

"He's being litter trained. And, of course, he has all his shots, and has been neutered. He's hungry for attention—very affectionate and playful, now that he's feeling well. I think Jamie would enjoy him."

"I'm sure she would," Spence said, "but—"

"If you're worried about the dogs, they wouldn't bother it. They've been around cats—and other small animals—before."

"Libby," Spence said, trying to get her to hush a minute and let him talk. She'd obviously prepared her speech.

She fell silent. Probably out of arguments, he thought. "First off, I want to thank you for the offer—for wanting to do something nice for Jamie. I just don't think a pet's such a good idea right now."

A tiny frown appeared between her eyebrows. "Would you mind telling me why?"

He did mind, as a matter of fact. He hadn't had to explain his actions to anyone for a long time—especially when it came to the decisions he made about his kid. But he reminded himself of the eagerness in her face when she'd made the offer and forced himself to reply patiently. "For one thing, what would she do with it while she's at school all day?"

"Cats are quite self-sufficient," Libby answered immediately. "As long as she gives it attention when she's home, and makes sure it has fresh food and water and clean litter, it would be fine for a few hours alone each day—inside or outside. For that matter, I'm told that every barn needs a cat, to keep out the mice," she added with a smile.

"And what about when Jamie and I leave here next spring? I'm not sure we could take a cat on the road with us. An RV's close quarters for two people—not much room to spare for pets."

Something flashed through Libby's expression that Spence couldn't quite read. She glanced away before he had a chance to interpret it. "I hadn't thought about that," she admitted. "But I suppose it could always stay here, with us."

"Look, if you want to bring the cat home as your pet, that's your choice," Spence said a bit more bluntly than he'd intended. "Jamie'll probably get a kick out of it, which is fine as long as she doesn't get any ideas about it belonging to her. I don't want her getting too attached to, er, to anything while we're here."

Libby's gaze met his then, but he had no more success at reading her thoughts than when she'd been looking away. "I understand," she said.

He was uncomfortably concerned that she *did* understand.

She changed the subject rather abruptly. "How are things going at the Hollister ranch?"

He shrugged and turned to put away the pitchfork. "Fine. Chuck likes what I've been doing with his Appaloosa. Said he's got a couple of friends who've been looking for a good trainer. He's going to recommend me to them."

Libby nodded. "Sounds like you've got your work lined up for you."

Just in case she was concerned, he assured her, "My work here comes first. I won't neglect any of the chores you're paying me to do."

"I'm sure you won't. I'm very pleased with your work, Spence."

He grunted in reply, not at all certain that he liked having her speak to him in such an employer-to-employee manner. He didn't really know why it bothered him; after all, she *was* his employer. Nothing more.

Absently Libby rocked her foot against the railing, causing the stall door to swing back and forth. A squeal of protest came from one of the hinges.

Spence scowled, taking the squeak personally. "I'll put some oil on that first thing in the morning."

She stopped swinging the gate and stepped away from it. "Okay."

Spence wondered why she was still hanging around. Was there something else she wanted to say to him? If so, she was taking her sweet time about it.

The silence between them lengthened. He cleared his throat. "I haven't seen you around much in the past couple of weeks," he commented, just to have something to say. "Guess you've been pretty busy at work."

"Yes. Our practice is growing almost faster than we can keep up with it."

"That's good for business, I guess."

"Hell on a social life, though," Libby murmured, then smiled as though at a private joke.

Not for the first time, Spence wondered about her social life. If she was dating anyone in particular, she certainly never brought him around. He'd seen her leave the house one evening in a glittery cocktail dress that had made him stare in surprise at her intriguing transformation from no-frills veterinarian to alluring woman, but she'd left alone and returned the same way soon after midnight.

He'd just happened to be awake to notice her return. He assured himself now—as he had then—that he hadn't really been waiting up for her.

Her business partner had stopped by the house a couple of times, but Gran had told him that Baker was a happily married man. After surreptitiously watching them together, Spence didn't think there was anything going on between the two vets.

So was there some other reason she spent so much time alone?

"You ever been married?" he asked, then wondered in exasperation why he'd spoken the thought aloud.

Libby's eyebrows rose. "No," she said after a moment. "I guess there just hasn't been time. I haven't ruled it out, though."

He busied himself stowing the tack he'd cleaned and oiled earlier. "Just curious," he said gruffly. "You seem to like kids."

"Yes, I do. And as Gran keeps reminding me, I'm not getting any younger. But I still have a few childbearing years left," she added with a trace of humor.

Spence's mouth quirked in a faint smile. "A few. What are you—twenty-five? Twenty-six?"

"Thank you. I'm twenty-nine."

He was surprised, but didn't allow it to show. He was not surprised by her desire to have children. Whatever other regrets Spence might have about his own life, Jamie had never been one of them. He wouldn't trade his role as her dad for the biggest purse in rodeo. He thought it would be a shame if Libby Carter never had kids; he bet she'd make a great mother. With a few modifications, of course.

"Having kids would sure cut into those god-awful work hours of yours," he commented.

"I know I need to cut down on my hours," Libby admitted. "Paul and I have already discussed taking on a new partner. But having a family wouldn't mean I couldn't still do my work. I know lots of successful career women who also have families."

Spence thought bitterly of one woman who had been forced into a choice between her career and her family, and hadn't chosen family. "From what I've seen, it's damned hard to mix a demanding career and a family. One or the other almost always suffers from too little time and too little attention."

"Is that what happened to you, Spence? Did your ex-wife choose career over family?"

He opened his mouth, then shut it with a snap, stunned to realize that he had almost told her the whole story.

What the hell? He *never* talked about his ex-wife— as far as he was concerned she might as well have died five years ago when she'd walked out on him and their daughter. He could see no purpose that could be served by talking of her, and especially not to Libby.

Maybe he just didn't want Libby to know what a loser he really was.

He made a show of looking at his watch. "Damn," he said. "I'd better get back to the house. It's time for Jamie to turn off the TV and get ready for bed."

To his relief, Libby didn't press for an answer to her question. She only nodded and moved toward the barn door.

Spence wasn't sure what made him reach out and catch her shoulder to delay her. Maybe it was the way she'd avoided his eyes as she'd turned away from him. "Libby?"

He heard her breath hitch in a soft sound when he touched her, felt the way her muscles stiffened fractionally beneath his hand. He knew she wasn't afraid of him. But she *was* aware of him. Just as he was suddenly aware of her. Of the way her short curls lay against the back of her neck. Of the fresh, clean scent of her. Of the warmth of her skin through the thin fabric of her blouse. He couldn't help wondering if that warm skin was as soft as it looked. Or if her intriguingly shaped mouth tasted as sweet as he suspected.

He'd been too long without a woman, he thought grimly. Or maybe there was something about this woman that tempted him to forget the hard lessons he'd learned from others.

She slanted him a look from beneath her lashes, making him realize how long and dark they were. How intriguingly they shadowed her flushed cheeks. "Was there something else you wanted, Spence?" she asked.

The innocently provocative wording made him swallow hard. Or *had* it been innocent? Something about the way she was looking at him . . .

"Uh, yeah. Thank you again for wanting to do something nice for Jamie. You know—by giving her the kitten. Sorry it didn't work out."

"So am I," she said quietly. "If you change your mind, you still have a couple of days to let me know. I want to keep it at the clinic until I'm sure it's completely well."

He nodded and released her. She didn't immediately step away. Her lashes lifted, so that she was looking straight into his eyes. And this time he didn't think he was imagining the sensual awareness in her gaze.

"Good night, Spence," she said, her voice a bit huskier than usual.

He watched her mouth as she shaped the words, then continued to stare at it when he replied, "G'night, Libby."

She moistened her lips with the tip of her tongue. Subconsciously? Or because he was staring at them? Damn, but he suddenly wanted to taste her more than he wanted his next breath.

Libby turned and was gone before he could figure out when the hell he'd started thinking of his employer as an intriguingly desirable woman. Had it been the night he'd seen her in that clinging, sexy cocktail dress? Or had it begun even before that, when he'd noticed what a nice smile she had?

Not that he planned to do anything about it, of course. He didn't go looking for trouble these days.

JAMIE WAS DRESSED in her favorite Aladdin-and-Jasmine nightshirt. Her teeth had been brushed, her prayers said. Spence tucked the covers around her and the ragged stuffed bear she'd been sleeping with since she was two.

"You feeling okay, honey?" he asked, lingering for a moment beside the bed and studying her grave little face in the soft glow of the night-light. "You've been awfully quiet this evening."

Jamie sighed. "Jennifer Beckles wasn't at school today."

Spence frowned, trying to make a connection. "She wasn't?"

"No. Mrs. Bennett said it was 'cause Jennifer's grandmother died yesterday."

"Oh. That's a shame."

When Jamie didn't say anything else for several moments, Spence asked, "Are you sad for your friend?"

Jamie nodded against the pillow.

Feeling awkward, Spence touched his daughter's cheek. "She'll be okay, punkin. It hurts to lose someone, but it gets a little easier as time goes by. We've talked about this before, remember? Death is just a natural part of life."

"I know. Jennifer's grandmother is in heaven now, and that's a special place where everyone's happy."

"Right." Hoping he'd somehow managed to comfort her, he leaned over to kiss her again. "Good night, Jamie."

"'Night, Dad."

Spence had made it to the door before Jamie spoke again. "Dad?"

"What is it, baby?"

"Gran's pretty old, isn't she?"

So that's what this is about. "She's certainly not young anymore, Jamie," he answered carefully. "But she's very healthy for her age. Remember I said just yesterday that she seems to have a lot more energy than I do at times?"

"I remember. I just wouldn't want anything to happen to *my* Gran."

Spence was tempted to remind her that Emma Grandjean wasn't *her* Gran. That Jamie had only known the woman for a couple of months. But something made him hold his tongue. "We'll, uh, we'll watch out for her while we're here, okay?" he said instead.

That seemed to reassure the child. "Right. She'll be okay as long as you're taking care of her, won't she?"

Spence sighed, both touched and disturbed by his daughter's misplaced confidence in him. No matter how many times he screwed up, no matter how many problems they encountered, Jamie was still utterly confident that he could make everything work out all right. He wished he had as much faith in himself. But he wasn't about to promise that he could personally keep anything bad from happening to Mrs. Grandjean—or anyone else, for that matter.

"You included Gran in your prayers tonight, didn't you?" he asked instead.

"Sure. I always do. Libby, too. And Sherman and Peabody and Tennessee and Alabama. And Jennifer Beckles and Mrs. Bennett, and Grandmother Holiday and Grandpa Holiday and Linda and Tina, and Slick and K.C. and—"

Spence cut firmly into the recitation of friends, family and animals. No wonder Jamie always took so long to whisper her prayers! He couldn't help wondering if she ever included her long-gone mother in her list.

"Okay, kid, I get the picture," he said. "The point is that you've turned Gran's welfare over to a higher authority. So you really shouldn't worry about it anymore tonight, all right?"

Jamie thought about it a moment, then nodded again, more confidently this time. "You're right, Dad. Nothing I can do by worrying, is there?"

"Not a thing," he assured her.

"Can I have blueberry muffins for breakfast in the morning?"

"*May* I," Spence corrected, bemused but not surprised by the typically rapid change of subject and mood. "And, yeah, you can. If we've got any mix left, that is."

"Okay. 'Night."

He stepped outside the room, shaking his head.

LIBBY WAS STANDING in her kitchen, rinsing out a coffee cup, ready to turn in for the evening, when she heard the light rap on the kitchen door. Surprised, she stepped over to open it. It was much too late for Jamie to be up and about—even Gran had been in bed for a couple of hours already. But why would Spence be knocking at this hour?

She opened the door to find out.

Illuminated by the yellow bulb above the door, Spence frowned. "You really should ask who it is before you open the door."

"You're right," Libby admitted, rather surprised that she had just assumed it was Spence. She wasn't usually so incautious. "Is something wrong, Spence?"

He shifted his feet on the low step outside the door, looking uncomfortable. He wasn't wearing his black hat now, and his dark hair was rumpled around his face as though he'd been running a hand through it. He was still wearing the chambray shirt and jeans he'd had on when she'd seen him earlier, in the barn. A dark stubble shadowed his jaw and upper lip, accentuating his raw masculinity.

"Is your offer of the cat for Jamie still open?"

She hadn't expected that. He'd sounded so adamant when he'd refused earlier. "Yes, of course. But . . ."

He shrugged, obviously not wanting her to make a big deal of his change of mind. "I know a few ropers who travel with dogs. Guess a cat wouldn't be much trouble."

"Oh." She wished she understood him better. He didn't look particularly happy about accepting the offer. Why *had* he changed his mind? "Have you told Jamie?"

"No. You can surprise her if you want. She'd probably get a kick of out it."

"All right. I'll bring the kitten home one evening next week."

"Fine." He nodded, then turned away, apparently intending to leave without another word.

Libby spoke impulsively. "Spence?"

He looked over his shoulder. "Yeah?"

"Would you, uh, like to come in for a drink or something?"

He looked past her into the kitchen. "Your grandmother still awake?"

"No. She's been in bed awhile."

His expression was impossible to read. "I'd better not."

Libby nodded, trying not to show that she was disappointed. "I suppose you want to get back to Jamie."

"Jamie's fine. She's asleep."

"Then—"

"I just don't know if it's a good idea for you and me to get involved in anything right now."

"You *what?*" she asked when she was sure she could speak coherently again. Maybe she'd misunderstood him.

But she hadn't. "I work for you," Spence explained, his expression carved in granite. "That can get awkward enough without having your grandmother and my daughter so close all the time. And I'll be moving on come spring, so—"

"Are you actually insinuating," Libby cut in flatly, "that you think I was making a pass when I invited you in for a drink?"

Spence seemed to notice her expression then. He cleared his throat and shuffled his boots on the concrete step. "No offense," he muttered, "but—"

Libby slammed the kitchen door shut in his face. Then, for good measure, she snapped off the outside light, leaving him standing alone in the darkness. She whirled to leave the room, fuming. Of all the arrogant, conceited, ill-bred, uncalled for . . .

The door opened behind her. She'd forgotten to lock it.

"Look," Spence said, "I didn't mean to make you mad. I was just—"

"Get out of my house." She never even looked around.

"If you'd just let me—"

She kept walking. "Go to hell."

She couldn't remember being this angry with anyone in a very long time. If ever. Maybe she *had* overreacted, but for him to actually think, and even to come right out and say, that she had chased after him like some bubbly, bleached-permed-and-teased rodeo groupie . . . She'd never been so insulted in her life.

A hard, strong hand fell on her shoulder, effectively stopping her in her tracks before she could reach the doorway. "Damn it, Libby, if you'd just wait a minute and let me try to explain," Spence roared, seeming to forget that they weren't alone in the house.

"Explain what?" she asked him just as heatedly, tossing him a furious look over her shoulder. "That you're an egotistical, ill-mannered jerk? I figured that out all by myself, thank you."

"I wasn't trying to insult you!"

"Well, you did a hell of a job of it, anyway!"

He glared at her, his nose only inches from hers. "Don't you think you're making too big a deal out of this?"

"Just because you accused me of throwing myself at you? Gee, I guess that's not such a big deal, after all."

Spence closed his eyes and drew in a deep breath, obviously striving for patience. "I didn't say you were throwing yourself at me," he said finally, opening his eyes again to look relentlessly into her own. "You haven't done anything of the sort. Maybe I was wrong, but I thought you were attracted to me—the same way I've been attracted to you for the past couple of weeks. If I've offended you, I'm sorry."

Libby stared at him. "You're attracted to me?"

His hard mouth quirked at the question. "Yeah."

She wondered when *that* had happened. She was quite sure he hadn't been taken with her as quickly as she had been with him. When had he started to notice her?

"Is it really all that bad?" she couldn't help asking.

He grimaced. "Probably. You have to understand that I'm not looking for any long-term involvements."

Her temper simmered again. "And just who said I was?"

"Don't be so touchy. No one said you were—hell, especially not with someone like me. I just—"

"What do you mean, 'someone like you'?"

"Do you *ever* let anyone finish a damned sentence?" he exploded in visible frustration.

She bit her lip. "Sorry."

Spence exhaled through his nose and shoved a hand through his hair. "I don't know how the hell we got into all this. But there are a lot of good reasons why you and I should keep our relationship strictly professional."

Damned if the man wasn't harder on her ego—and her temper—than any man she'd ever known. "You think so, do you?" she said quietly.

"Yeah." He looked relieved that they were no longer shouting.

She nodded, keeping her expression cool. "No problem. But there is just one little thing you seem to have overlooked, Spencer."

He frowned warily at her clipped use of his full last name. "What little thing?"

"You're assuming this inconvenient attraction you've been feeling is mutual. A rather arrogant presumption on your part, wouldn't you say?"

With that, she lifted her chin with all the icy hauteur of royalty and moved to sweep out of the room. "You can let yourself out," she dismissed him. "I'm going to bed."

She didn't even take a complete step. Before she'd realized his intentions, Spence spun her into his arms, jerked her firmly against the unyielding wall of his chest and crushed her mouth beneath his own.

The kiss emptied her mind, melted her backbone and turned her knees to Jell-O. All those wonderful, heady, exciting things that no man's kiss had ever done for her before except in vague fantasies. He wasn't gentle, he wasn't chivalrous, and he wasn't particularly smooth. But by the time he finally released her mouth, she knew there was no lingering doubt in either of their minds that the attraction was very definitely mutual.

She was plastered against him like a temporary tattoo. She blushed hotly and jerked herself away from him. "That was—"

"Unplanned," he admitted. "But interesting."

"You—"

"Had better leave," he finished for her with a nod. "Before things get out of hand."

"Stop finishing my sentences for me!"

"Annoying habit, isn't it?" he asked and his sudden grin made her long to hit him—and then to drag him to the floor and throw herself all over him, damn it.

He leaned over and kissed her again, so quickly there wasn't time to respond had she tried. "You really shouldn't frown so much, Libby. You'll get wrinkles. Good night."

He was whistling when he let himself out the kitchen door, leaving her staring after him, amazed that he was suddenly in such a good mood. Why on earth?

"Libby?" Gran's voice floated down from the top of the stairs. "Is everything all right down there? I heard voices."

"Go back to bed, Gran. Everything's fine," Libby called back automatically. "I'm just locking up."

But everything *wasn't* fine, of course. Everything was very strange. And Libby found herself suddenly very, very nervous.

7

IT WAS AFTER eight o'clock by the time Libby arrived home from work Wednesday evening, five days after her confrontation with Spence. She had planned to leave the clinic at five, and had actually been on the way out the door when she'd been detained by an emergency.

A seven-year-old cocker spaniel had dashed in front of a car and been run over. Its frantic owners, a couple in their late fifties, had brought it to Libby, tearfully asking her to save their pet. She'd given them little hope when she'd first seen it.

The poor thing had been in bad shape, so bad that she thought there was no recourse but euthanasia. After a closer examination, she'd been able to offer a guarded chance that the dog could survive—but only after lengthy and expensive surgical repairs. The owners had brushed aside any concerns about money, telling her they didn't care what it cost, they wanted her to try everything she could.

The painstaking operation had taken nearly two hours. When it was over, Libby was exhausted, but much more confident the dog would live. She'd sat with it for a while after the surgery, then sent the couple home, promising their pet would be carefully monitored. She'd brushed off their effusive thanks, telling them she'd rather they would wait to thank her until they were all certain the dog would live.

She climbed heavily from behind the wheel of the Explorer, her entire body complaining. She tried not to think about the night ahead. She'd want to check on the spaniel again at least once, maybe twice. She'd try to eat and shower and get a couple of hours' rest between trips to the clinic.

She walked around her vehicle and opened the hatchback. Reaching inside, she pulled out a small animal carrier. A plaintive meow came from inside it.

"It's okay, sweetie," Libby crooned to the jittery kitten. "You'll be home soon."

Holding the carrier in one hand, she dragged out a large plastic bag with the other, setting the bag at her feet while she closed the back of the Explorer. And then she retrieved the bag and headed for the cottage, steeling herself for the imminent encounter with Spence. She hadn't talked to him since that night in her kitchen, having seen him only long enough to nod in passing during the days since. She'd tried to put his kisses out of her mind as completely as she'd stayed out of his sight. She had failed.

She would deliver the kitten to Jamie, treat Spence politely but rather coolly, and then go to her own house for dinner. She would give him no reason to accuse her of throwing herself at him again. Her ego still smarted from her last unnerving clash with him.

Spence answered the door when she knocked. He studied her for a moment in the harsh glow of the porch light, then further bruised her ego by saying bluntly, "You look like hell."

She sighed. "Thank you so much for pointing that out."

"You're just getting home from work?"

"Yes. There was a last-minute emergency—a dog hit by a car."

"You look like the car hit you instead."

She tapped her foot against the porch, beginning to get annoyed. "Are you quite through insulting me now?"

He looked faintly surprised. "I wasn't insulting you. I'm concerned about you. You look like you could keel over any minute."

Spence was *concerned* about her? Despite her exasperation with his tactless manner of expressing himself, she couldn't help but soften at his admission. "Oh. Well—I'm fine, Spence, really. Just tired."

"Come in and have a drink. You look like you could use, er, I mean, maybe it would make you feel a little better."

She couldn't help laughing. "Anyone ever call you a silver-tongued charmer, Spence?"

"No," he admitted with a rueful grin.

"I didn't think so."

He seemed to suddenly notice that both her hands were full. He reached immediately for the animal carrier. "Here, let me take that. I assume it's the cat for Jamie?"

"Yes. Is she here?"

"She ran over to your house to get her Barbie doll. She left it over there earlier when she was spending the afternoon with your grandmother. Come on in and sit down a minute. I told her not to be long, so she should be right back."

Libby had been counting on Jamie's presence to diffuse the tension between herself and Spence. She cleared her throat and indicated the plastic bag in her hand. "I've brought a few supplies for the kitten—a litter pan, litter, some food, a couple of kitty toys. Where do you want me to put them?"

"Just set it anywhere." Spence peered through the air holes molded into the plastic carrier. "The cat looks scared to death."

"The trip probably made it nervous. He'll be fine once he settles down. We'll have to warn Jamie that he may scratch at first if she isn't careful. He loves being petted and cuddled and has had plenty of handling at the clinic, but he'll be jumpy for the first couple of days after being resettled. It's normal."

Spence set the carrier carefully on the floor beside the plastic bag Libby had deposited just inside the door. "I'll tell her to be careful, but it probably won't be necessary. That kid has a real thing with animals. She loves them and they seem to know it and return the feeling."

"I've noticed that with the dogs," Libby admitted, perching on the edge of the couch. "She told me again the other day that she wants to be a vet. I told her she'd be a natural at the job."

Spence half sat, half leaned on the arm of the couch. "That must have pleased her."

"Yes, it seemed to."

"What do you want to drink? I've got soda, milk, instant coffee or juice. I'd offer something stronger, but I don't keep liquor in the house. Doesn't set a good example for Jamie."

She stifled a smile, afraid that he'd take it the wrong way. Spence's concern for his daughter didn't amuse her—just the opposite, actually. She admired him greatly for it. Whatever other problems this complex cowboy might have, he was a good father to his little girl. "Soda will be fine, thank you."

Spence pushed himself to his feet. "I'll be right back."

Jamie burst into the house before Spence returned with Libby's drink. "Hi, Libby!" she said, her face lighting up with her smile as she rushed to greet her guest. "What are you doing here?"

Libby reached out to give the child a quick hug. "I brought you a present," she said.

Jamie's eyes rounded with excitement. "You did?"

Spence came back into the room, carrying a glass of soda in each hand. He gave one to Libby, then settled into an armchair with his own. "Look in the plastic box, Jamie," he advised, nodding toward the pet carrier in the corner.

Jamie approached the carrier carefully. Spence and Libby exchanged smiling glances when the child knelt to peer in through the holes. The kitten meowed just as Jamie bent close.

Jamie caught her breath. "A kitten? Is it a kitten, Libby?"

"Open the door and see," Libby advised her. "But move slowly so you don't frighten it."

Jamie opened the door and looked inside the carrier. "Oh," she breathed. "It's beautiful!" Carefully she reached into the box, crooning softly to the nervous kitten. "Come on, little kitty. I won't hurt you. I'm going to take care of you."

Libby held her breath, hoping the kitten didn't scratch Jamie's hand. She let the breath out in relief when Jamie lifted the tiny animal with exquisite care and snuggled it against her little chest. The kitten burrowed against her as though it knew it was coming home, its four tiny white feet curled beneath its fluffy little gray body.

"I told you Jamie's got a thing with animals," Spence murmured, shaking his head. "Never saw anything like it."

It really was rather amazing how instantly the kitten took to Jamie. Within minutes it was purring and rubbing against her chin, eagerly demanding her attention. Libby couldn't help laughing softly. The cat should be hiding under the furniture, taking its own time getting to know the new surroundings and new humans around it.

Jamie looked up from the kitten with a glowing smile. "She's wonderful," she said. "Thank you, Libby. Thank you so much for giving her to me."

"Him," Libby corrected. "The kitten's a male."

Jamie didn't seem perturbed by the change of gender. "Then I'll have to think of a boy's name for him. He doesn't already have a name, does he?"

"No. I thought you'd like to name him."

Jamie had already turned to her father. "May I keep him, Dad? Please? I'll take good care of him, I promise."

"You can keep him," Spence assured her.

"Wow. Thanks, Daddy. I love him. Can he sleep with me?"

"We'll talk about that later. Why don't you take him into the kitchen and give him some water and some food. Libby brought supplies for him. They're in the bag beside the carrier."

"You'll want to set his litter box up quickly and show him where it is," Libby advised. "And you need to change the litter often—for the kitten's sake and for your father's," she added with a smile.

Jamie nodded fervently. "Okay. C'mon, kitty, let's go check out your new home. Would you like some milk? I can pour you some. Or maybe—"

She was still talking when the kitchen door swung closed behind her.

"I think the cat was a hit," Spence said dryly.

"I think you're right. I'm glad he has a good home."

"You get lots of strays?"

"Yes, I'm afraid so. Thoughtless people are always dumping them at the clinic doorstep. We find homes for as many as we can, but of course it isn't always possible. Some have to be put to sleep. If only pet owners would be responsible enough to have their animals neutered so there wouldn't be all these unwanted litters to—"

She stopped abruptly, grimacing self-consciously. "Sorry. I didn't mean to get on my soapbox."

"It's okay. You don't want to be around when I start talking about people who buy a half-acre of land, then decide that's enough to put a horse or a pony on."

Libby frowned. "I know what you mean. I see that all the time, especially out in rural areas. There's a mobile home a few miles down the road with two ponies fenced into a tiny lot barely large enough to keep a big dog in. There's no grass, and every time it rains the ground turns to deep mud. It's pathetic. The same people keep a German shepherd short-chained to a tree in their front yard. I stopped once to introduce myself, but when I started talking about the health of their animals they became very belligerent and told me to leave."

Spence was scowling. "Jerks."

"Yes. They are."

They sat in companionable silence for a few minutes, sipping their sodas and listening to Jamie talking to the kitten in the other room. And then Libby sighed and rose to her feet. "I'd better go," she said. "I haven't even seen Gran yet, and I'd like to grab a bite to eat before I drive back to the clinic."

Spence's frown deepened. "You're going back to the clinic tonight?"

She nodded. "I have a patient to check on—the emergency I told you about. He'll have to be checked at least once tonight, maybe twice."

"You don't need to be out on the roads alone in the middle of the night."

She shrugged. "I'll be okay. I have a dependable vehicle with a built-in telephone, and I keep my doors locked."

"Let me know when you're ready to go and I'll ride along."

"That's not necessary. I do this often."

Spence shook his head. "Not tonight. You never know who could be lurking around the clinic waiting for you to show up."

"Who would know I was coming—or when?" she asked logically.

"Well, someone could be trying to get in to steal drugs or something. It's just too dangerous for you to go alone. I'll go with you."

"No, Spence. There's no—"

"Either you promise to tell me when you're leaving or I'll just watch your car until I see you come out and then I'll follow you."

His expression was inflexible. Libby planted her hands on her hips, not quite believing they were having this conversation. "And what about your daughter? You would be leaving her here alone."

"She can go with us."

"Spence, it will be the middle of the night! Jamie has school tomorrow. She needs her rest. Now please stop being so stubborn and believe me when I tell you that I'm perfectly capable of taking care of myself. I won't have you leaving a ten-year-old child here alone so you can ride with me on a routine run to my office."

She could tell she finally had him caught in a stalemate, torn between his concern for her and his responsibility to his daughter. She stepped closer to him and placed a hand on his rigid arm. "I'll be fine, really. But thank you for being concerned about me."

He wrapped one hand around her neck and tugged her closer. "You be careful," he growled.

"I will," she whispered, aware of his mouth so very close to her own, remembering the way it had felt pressed so tightly to hers.

And then he kissed her again, driving the memory of those other kisses to the back of her mind so that she could concentrate fully on this one. The kiss was brief, but thorough. She was trembling when it ended.

"You really should stop doing that," she said when she was sure she could speak without stammering.

"Yeah, I should," he agreed, his expression unreadable. "But I probably won't."

She took a step backward. "Anyone ever tell you you're just a tiny bit arrogant, Michael Spencer?"

His hard mouth quirked in what might have been a smile. "No. No one's ever said anything about it being a 'tiny bit.'"

She was still too shaken to laugh. "Good night, Spence," she said with all the dignity she had left—a woefully small amount, unfortunately.

"Use that built-in phone if you need me," he said.

She only nodded and made her exit as swiftly as possible.

GRAN FUSSED OVER LIBBY from the minute she walked into the house, chiding her for working so hard, fretting that she hadn't yet eaten, bemoaning the need for her to go out again. She knew better than to try to talk her out of it, of course. Gran had long since accepted Libby's devotion to her job, even if she did feel obliged to make her token protests.

Libby gave her grandmother's lecture only half her attention as she gratefully ate the stew and biscuits Gran had kept warm for her. The other half of her attention kept wandering to Spence—and his kisses—no matter how desperately she tried to keep herself from thinking about him.

"Did you hear me, Libby?" Gran asked, obviously not for the first time.

Libby blinked and looked up from her almost-finished dinner. "I'm sorry, Gran, what did you say?"

Her grandmother sighed, but repeated patiently, "My friend Sylvia in Branson, Missouri, has offered to put us up in her bed-and-breakfast for a weekend in early December. She'll pull strings to get us into some of the best shows and she said everything will be decorated for the holidays. It sounds wonderful."

"You should go, Gran. It should be a lot of fun."

"Not me—*we*," Gran corrected. "The offer includes you."

Libby frowned. "But that's only a little more than a month away."

"Right. You need this time off, Libby. Please think about it."

"I just don't know if I can manage it right now. Everything gets so hectic during the holidays, and Paul's busy with building his new house and—"

"Paul had his vacation last month," Gran reminded her firmly. "And he promised to take care of everything whenever you were ready to take some time off for yourself. The clinic can get along without you for a few days, Libby."

Libby was still shaking her head. "I don't know, Gran. But I'll think about it," she promised.

Her grandmother looked far from satisfied. "You do that," she grumbled. "You think very hard about it. You need this time off."

Libby decided to change the subject. "Are you still going to Hot Springs with your Sunday school class next Friday night?"

"Yes. We're going to shop at the outlet mall, and go up in the observation tower, eat at Coy's and then spend the night at the Arlington. Would you like to go with us, dear?"

Libby smiled at the thought of being on a church bus for a weekend with eleven septuagenarians. "It sounds like a lot of fun, Gran, but I think I'll pass this time."

"You'll think about Branson?" Gran persisted with her single-minded stubbornness.

"I'll think about it," Libby promised once more, then changed the subject again by telling Gran of Jamie's delight at receiving the kitten. That diversion proved successful; Gran was crazy about little Jamie and was pleased to hear that the kitten had been such a hit. The Branson vacation was forgotten; Libby hoped to keep it that way for a while. She really didn't have time to take a vacation for the next few months, she thought. She'd take some time off as soon as she could, she silently promised her grandmother. Soon.

IT WAS AFTER MIDNIGHT when Libby left for her clinic. She quietly shut the front door behind her, shivering a little as the cool air of the night closed around her. It would be winter soon, she thought, breathing deeply of the crisp fragrance of autumn. Funny how fast the time was speeding past her as she approached her thirtieth birthday, she mused with a grimace.

She burrowed more deeply into her lightweight denim jacket and walked toward her Explorer, her boots making quiet, crunching noises on the gravel driveway. She had her hand on the door handle when she realized she wasn't alone.

Her heart in her throat, she whirled to stare at the man who'd approached her so silently. "Damn it, Spence, you scared me half to death," she scolded him, recognizing him in the glow of the security lights.

"Good," he said without apology. "Maybe that will remind you to be on your guard while you're out by yourself at night."

She shook her head, her pulse still racing in reaction to the start he'd given her. "Of all the—"

"How long you think you'll be gone?"

"I don't know. Why?"

"Give me a time. If you're not back by then, I'm calling the cops."

She rolled her eyes heavenward. "And if I'm held up by an emergency?"

"Then you can call and let me know," he said succinctly. "Give me a time, Libby."

She exhaled in frustration, but muttered, "Forty minutes." It was a ten-minute drive to her clinic; that left her twenty minutes to check on the spaniel and the other animals. She figured that would be plenty of time.

He nodded. "All right. Lock your doors."

"I will. But it really isn't necessary for you to wait up until I get back. I'm sure you need your rest."

"So do you. So get going. The quicker you get back, the sooner both of us can get to bed."

She shook her head at his obstinacy, refusing to dwell on her sudden mental image of both of them in bed—together. She climbed behind the steering wheel and closed the door firmly in Spence's face.

He tapped on the window. "Lock the doors," he ordered through the glass. "And fasten your seat belt."

"Go to hell," she muttered, but complied with both instructions before turning the key in the ignition.

"I heard that." He'd lifted his voice to be heard over the engine.

She gave him an overly sweet smile through the window. "I meant for you to." And then she threw the vehicle into gear and drove away, leaving him standing in the shadowy driveway, looking after her.

She was sure he meant well. But she already had a grandmother. She didn't need another one. That wasn't the sort of relationship she wanted with Spence, anyway.

SHE WAS BACK HOME in thirty-five minutes. Spence stood in the open doorway of the cottage, making sure she saw him in the beam of the porch light. He didn't come out to meet her, but lifted a hand to acknowledge her safe arrival and then disappeared inside his house, closed his door behind him and turned off the lights.

Libby didn't know whether she wanted more badly to hit him, or to kiss him silly. But she glumly suspected that it was the latter option she found more tempting.

8

THE FOLLOWING WEEK, Spence found himself alone on a Friday evening, unenthusiastically considering what he wanted to eat for dinner. Jamie was spending the night with her friend, Patty, and the cottage seemed quiet and empty without her in it.

A plaintive meow sounded from the floor. Spence looked down at the kitten winding itself around his feet. "You miss her, too, huh?"

The cat jumped lightly onto Spence's knee and butted against his hand. Spence gave in to the less-than-subtle hint and rubbed its pointed ears, resulting in a noisy, rumbling purr.

Music drifted from the radio on the kitchen counter; Spence had turned it on when the the quiet had gotten on his nerves. He listened to an old Garth Brooks tune as he patted the kitten and contemplated how dull his life had become. Here he was, single, thirty-three years old and free for a Friday evening, and he could think of nothing he wanted to do. The thought of going to a bar or to a restaurant alone didn't appeal to him; there were no movies he wanted to see, no errands he needed to run.

He'd met a few available women during the past few months, mostly single mothers with kids the same age as Jamie. A couple of them had let him know in various ways that they wouldn't mind if he asked them out. He couldn't work up any enthusiasm about calling any of them.

When had he started to live like such a monk? True, there hadn't been a lot of opportunities to go out since he'd become solely responsible for Jamie. But there'd been other evenings, like tonight, when she'd stayed over with friends or had other plans. He'd usually made good use of the free time, rarely having any trouble finding a few hours of temporarily satisfying, undemanding female companionship. So what was holding him back tonight?

His attention was caught by the opening strains of an old Earl Thomas Conley tune, "What I'd Say." The song told of a man holding imaginary conversations with the woman who'd left him, rehearsing what he might say if he ran into her again. Should he talk about the weather, or let her know how badly she'd hurt him, how much he'd missed her? Would he tell her that he still loved her, yet somehow hated her at the same time? Should he say she was looking well, or should he tell her to go to hell?

Spence grimaced. Man, how many times had he listened to that one after Delilah had walked out on him? How many times had he wondered what *he* would say if he ran into her again? How many times had he asked himself whether he'd tell her to go to hell—or beg her to come back to him?

He still didn't know what he'd say if she showed up on his doorstep tomorrow. He wanted to think he'd tell her to get lost—but he wasn't entirely sure he had ever really gotten over her, damn it. He only knew that she had almost destroyed him when she'd left him. If it hadn't been for Jamie . . . He winced and made himself stop thinking along those painful lines.

A quick tap-tap on the kitchen door provided welcome distraction from his memories. He tipped the kitten off his knee and crossed the room to open the door. Libby stood outside, dressed in a black sweater and jeans with black boots, giving him a bland smile that dared him to say anything to make her uncomfortable. She held up a shapely blond doll. "Jamie left her Barbie at our house again," she said. "I thought I'd save her a trip and return it to her."

Spence reached out and took the doll. "Thanks. I'll give it to her tomorrow. She's spending the night with a friend tonight."

"Gran's gone for the evening, too. She's in Hot Springs with her Sunday school class."

Spence had forgotten that Mrs. Grandjean was gone for the evening. "So you're a bachelor tonight, too."

Libby smiled. "Yeah. I thought I'd crash in front of the TV with something fattening and totally nonnutritious—the sort of food Gran frowns at when she's home to monitor my diet."

Spence lifted an eyebrow. "You don't have a date or anything?"

She looked a bit self-conscious at the question, but lifted her chin. "No. Not tonight. How about you?"

"No," he admitted. "Tonight it's just me and Butch."

"Butch?" Libby inquired blankly.

"The cat."

"Oh." She was smiling again. "So that's what Jamie finally named him."

"Yeah. I talked her out of Buttercup. I was afraid the cat would get a complex or something if she stuck him with that one."

"You wouldn't believe some of the names people come up with for their pets," Libby told him with a laugh. Then she moved back from the door. "See you later, Spence."

He almost let her go. "Libby?"

She looked over her shoulder. "Yes?"

"Would you like to, uh, maybe do something tonight?"

Both her eyebrows rose in response to the awkwardly phrased question. "Do something?" she repeated.

"Yeah." He cursed himself for his clumsiness. One would think he'd never asked a woman out before. "You know, like maybe see a movie. Or go out to eat. Maybe share that nonnutritious meal in front of the TV."

Libby bit her lower lip. For the first time since Spence had met her, she looked a bit shy. "Okay."

"Okay?"

"Sure. Sounds nice."

"Which?"

She blinked. "Which what?"

"Which do you want to do?" he clarified. "See a movie? Go out to eat? Eat junk food and watch TV? Any combination of the above?"

"Oh." She pushed her hands into the pockets of her already-snug jeans, molding them more tightly against her slender hips. Spence tried not to notice. "It doesn't matter," she said. "Whatever you want to do."

He decided not to dwell too closely on what he would have liked to do with Libby. Thoughts like that could only lead to trouble. "Why don't we go out," he suggested, choosing what seemed to be the safest option. "Nothing fancy. There's no need to change. You look very nice the way you are."

"Thank you. Give me ten minutes to brush my hair and grab my purse, okay?"

"Make it fifteen. I'll put on a clean shirt."

"Fifteen minutes," she agreed and started walking toward her house.

Spence closed the kitchen door, then wasted five of his fifteen minutes wondering how he'd gotten himself into going on a Friday night date with his employer. This certainly wasn't the way he'd expected to spend the evening. But now that he'd made the commitment, he was rather looking forward to it.

SPENCE LEFT the choice of restaurants up to Libby, since she knew the area better than he did. He had become most familiar with places that catered to the under-twelve crowd.

Amused by his confession, Libby directed him to the Roundup, a popular new restaurant in west Little Rock with casual, down-home dining upstairs and a western dance club downstairs. The place was packed with wrangler wannabees in gaudy, designer western shirts, studded belts and ostrich-skin boots, women in peek-aboo western shirts and short denim skirts or skintight jeans worn with fringed leather boots.

Libby thought she blended well enough in her black, pirate-cut shirt and black jeans. Spence, however, looked rather out of place. In his simple white shirt with the mother-of-pearl snaps, neatly pressed jeans and newly polished boots, he looked like the only real cowboy in a room full of pretenders.

She wasn't the only one who noticed. More than one speculative woman and envious man glanced his way when a jeans-clad waitress led Spence and Libby to a table after a half-hour wait in the crowded bar.

"Interesting place you've brought me to," Spence drawled when they were seated. He was eyeing a rotund, florid-faced man poured into black jeans and the black-and-red "flames" western shirt that had been popular a year or so earlier after being favored by one member of a country singing duo. The wanna-be cowboy limped a little as he crossed the floor to the men's room; apparently his five-hundred-dollar boots pinched his chubby little toes.

Libby laughed at Spence's expression. "I thought you'd like it here."

"Mmm." His mutter was strictly noncommittal.

She took pity on him and admitted, "I brought you here for the food, Spence. The atmosphere may be tacky drugstore cowboy, but the menu is excellent. Best ribs in town. And Tex-Mex that will take the hair off your tongue."

Spence reached with more interest for his menu. "Now that sounds promising."

"Trust me," she said with a smile, lifting her own rope-bordered plastic menu.

Sometime later, Spence had to admit that Libby hadn't led him wrong. "This is great," he said after swallowing another bite of spicy beef-and-black-bean burrito.

"I'm glad you like it." Libby had just eaten the last of her chicken enchiladas. She couldn't decide if the food was especially good tonight, or if it just seemed better than usual because she was sharing it with Spence.

He'd proven to be a more amusing dinner companion than she'd expected. When he made an effort, Michael Spencer could be quite charming. He talked easily and entertainingly about a wide variety of subjects, though Libby was aware that he skillfully avoided divulging any personal information about himself. He loved talking about Jamie, but made no mention of his ex-wife, his family or his past, even when Libby tentatively tried to guide the conversation along those lines. There were so many things she wanted to know about him, so few things he was willing to reveal.

She tried to remind herself that this wasn't really a date—at least, not in the traditional sense. They weren't beginning a courtship or establishing a relationship. Spence had asked her out only because they'd both ended up alone for the evening, with no plans for dinner. Maybe he just hadn't wanted to eat alone; maybe he'd considered himself doing her a favor to offer companionship for the evening. But, oh, how she would have liked for it to be more than that!

She was getting involved, damn it. As hard as she'd fought it, as often as she'd warned herself that she was only going to get hurt if she wasn't careful, she was still drawn to him as she had been to no other man before him. She still found herself nursing foolish, secret fantasies that there could be a future for them, if only she could figure out how to break through that formidable reserve of his.

You can be such an idiot, Libby, she told herself in despair. And then she pushed such uncomfortable thoughts aside and allowed herself to concentrate only on the pleasure of being with Spence. Even if it were only for tonight.

THOUGH LIBBY TRIED to resist at first, Spence easily talked her into ordering dessert. She chose blackberry cobbler with ice cream; Spence selected chocolate peppermint pie. They lingered over the sweets, laughing about something cute Jamie had said at breakfast the morning before. Spence was rather surprised at how much he was enjoying the evening; it had been a long time since he'd spent such a pleasant, undemanding evening with an attractive woman.

A man's voice abruptly interrupted the conversation. "Libby?"

She looked over her shoulder, and then smiled. "Don! How nice to see you."

With a frown, Spence watched as the athletic-looking man in his mid-thirties leaned over to touch his lips to Libby's cheek. The interloper wore an expensive-looking blue sweater with pleated twill slacks and gleaming leather loafers, giving the appearance of a successful businessman out for an evening's relaxation. He had perfectly tanned skin, perfectly groomed blond hair and perfectly straight white teeth.

Spence didn't like him.

Libby obviously did. She was smiling at the guy like a long-lost friend, asking about his mother's health, his sister's new baby, if his law practice was doing well.

A lawyer, Spence thought glumly. Why wasn't he surprised?

After answering all Libby's questions, Don asked a few of his own. "How's Gran?" he wanted to know. "She still running around with that rowdy Sunday school class?"

Libby laughed. "She's in Hot Springs with them tonight." She described the active group's itinerary.

Spence thought about how much he hated hearing the guy call Mrs. Grandjean "Gran." Hell, even *he* called her Mrs. Grandjean, though she'd invited him several times to use the less formal nickname. He broodingly eyed the perfectly manicured male hand resting so familiarly on Libby's shoulder. Just how well did this guy know Libby? And if he was such a close friend, how come Spence hadn't seen him around during the past three months?

"Oh, I'm sorry. I'm completely forgetting my manners," Libby said suddenly, her cheeks going pink as she met Spence's eyes. "Michael Spencer, this is Don Cothren."

Cothren held out a hand, his smile looking relaxed and friendly. "Hi, Mike, nice to meet you."

Spence shook the guy's hand briefly, noting the difference between his hard, callused palm and Cothren's softer one. He made no effort to lie about how delighted he was to meet him.

A rather awkward silence followed. Cothren cleared his throat and stepped away from Libby, the hand that had been resting on her shoulder dropping to his side. Maybe he'd noticed how hard Spence had been looking at that wayward hand. "Well, uh, I'd better get back to my table. A group of us are here celebrating my law partner's fortieth birthday."

"It really was good to see you, Don."

Cothren shot a quick, measuring glance at Spence, then leaned over and deliberately brushed his mouth against Libby's. "You, too, Libby. You're looking good, by the way. Real good."

Her flush deepened. "Thank you."

Spence idly considered various methods of marring the guy's perfectly handsome face. Had he stopped to think about it, he might have wondered at this sudden streak of possessiveness he was feeling for a woman he'd been stoically trying to ignore the past few weeks. But he didn't stop to think about it. He just knew that if Cothren kissed her again, he would probably have to hurt him.

"Old school friend?" he asked when they were alone again.

"Someone I dated for a while, a couple of years ago," Libby corrected him, dipping her spoon into the remains of her dessert and evading Spence's eyes.

"You *dated* him?" Spence tried to sound mildly surprised.

"Yes. Why?"

He shrugged. "I wouldn't have thought he was your type."

Her eyebrow lifted. "And just what would you have said was my type?"

He shrugged again, deciding maybe it would be better not to get into that discussion. He swallowed the last bite of his pie and reached for his coffee cup to avoid answering.

Libby must have agreed that a change of subject was in order. "Why don't you use your first name?" she asked. "Have you always answered to Spence?"

"I answer to just about anything, including 'hey you,'" he replied casually. "But my dad started calling me Spence when I was just a toddler, and it stuck." He didn't add that, other than his mother, his ex-wife was the only one who'd ever called him Michael.

He really didn't need any reminders of Delilah tonight.

The silence lengthened and, again, it was Libby who seemed compelled to fill it. "I hear you've been getting quite a few calls about training horses," she said just a shade too heartily. "Chuck Hollister says you're about the best wrangler he's ever seen, and that's quite a compliment, believe me."

"Chuck's a decent guy. And, yeah, I've had a few calls. I'm going to follow up on a couple of them, see if I can work them in, but some I've had to turn down. I don't have time to take on many and still keep up with my other two jobs."

Libby frowned. "Is there really that much to do around our place? You've taken care of almost all the repairs, and the routine maintenance shouldn't take that much of your time. Don't feel that you have to keep yourself busy just to please Gran or me. You more than earn your salary, regardless of how many—or how few—hours it takes you to finish your chores. If you want to start a training business on the side, I certainly won't protest."

"I'm not starting a business of any kind," Spence said flatly. "I don't plan to stay long enough to make it profitable, and there's no need to start something I have no intention of pursuing."

He was uncomfortable again at talking salary and chores with Libby. It made him squirm to remember that technically she was his employer, that her money was at least partially supporting him and his daughter, that it was her roof over their heads at night. Maybe that was why he'd felt compelled to remind her that his position with her was only temporary, or maybe it had something to do with the surge of jealousy he'd felt when Don Cothren had leaned over to kiss her.

Libby's long lashes shielded the expression in her eyes as she pushed her dessert bowl away. "I can't eat another bite. But I enjoyed the dinner. I'm glad we came."

"The evening's not over yet," he reminded her, knowing he should probably take her on home and put some distance between them, aware that he wasn't quite ready to tell her good-night. "Why don't we work off some of this food on the dance floor downstairs?"

Libby looked surprised. "You dance?"

He scowled. "Of course I dance. Don't you?"

"Not very well. I'm not exactly up on the latest country line dances."

"I don't care much for line dances," Spence said, feeling himself suddenly starting to grin and not quite knowing why. "But I can two-step, Texas waltz and Cotton-eye Joe with the best of 'em."

Libby's smile returned slowly, but when it arrived it was worth the wait. He caught his breath in reaction to the gentle curve of her lips, the glimpse of teeth and tongue. "If you're willing to put up with an inexperienced partner, I'm game to try," she said.

Spence pushed his chair away from the table. "Then let's go."

LIBBY QUICKLY discovered that Spence hadn't been exaggerating about his dancing; he did that as well as he did everything else, with seemingly effortless grace and skill. He made no effort to follow the trends or impress anyone else on the dance floor. He simply had a good time, and made sure that Libby did, too.

The deejay was a well-known local radio personality. He played a nice selection of current hits and often-requested country "oldies." Spence and Libby two-stepped to an old Mickey Gilley tune, waltzed to George Strait's whiskey-smooth voice, even tried a couple of line dances, which Spence seemed to pick up quicker than Libby, despite his claim that he wasn't a line dance fan. She didn't care; she had a wonderful time. And when the deejay dimmed the dance floor lights and put on Mark Chestnutt's sultry "Almost Goodbye," Spence proved that he was even better at slow dancing than he had been with the faster steps.

He liked to dance close, her arms around his neck, his around her waist. His cheek rested against her hair and their legs brushed as he guided her in slow, rocking steps. He turned slightly, and Libby's breasts brushed his chest. She felt her nipples tighten in instinctive reaction.

Spence drew back a couple of inches so that he could look at her. She met his gaze with her own, trying to read his expression. He seemed to be studying her mouth; without thinking about it, she touched the tip of her tongue to her suddenly dry lower lip.

His arms tightened around her waist, drawing her even closer against his hard, warm body. She had to swallow a groan. Had any man ever felt this good, this right, in her arms? And they were only dancing. She could only imagine what it must be like to be held more intimately by him.

Spence lowered his head to press his lips against her temple. His breath was warm and moist against her skin. He brushed a kiss lower on her cheek, close to the corner of her mouth. She felt her heart leap into her throat. Her lips felt swollen, aching for the taste and the feel of his. He didn't make her wait long. His mouth settled firmly onto hers.

Libby didn't care who was watching them, didn't worry that they were being less than discreet. She'd never been less concerned with appearances or proprieties. She focused solely on the feel of Spence's arms around her, his chest against her breasts, his thighs pressed to hers. His kiss—so hot and demanding that she thought she might melt into an undignified puddle right there on the dance floor.

It was Spence who drew back, who seemed to become aware of their surroundings and their lack of privacy. But he didn't release her. Doug Stone's "Made for Loving You" was the next number played; Spence picked up the rhythm without a missed step. Libby nestled her cheek into his shoulder and followed more naturally than she'd ever danced in her life.

As though he sensed the swaying couples weren't quite ready to separate, the deejay played one more slow number—the late Keith Whitley crooning, "Don't Close Your Eyes." It was a sad song, a guy begging the woman in his arms not to think of the man in her past while he made love to her. Libby couldn't help wondering if Spence was thinking of anyone else now, while he held her so close, so tenderly.

Had he danced this way with the ex-wife who had hurt him so badly he couldn't even speak of her now? Did he still love her? Could he ever love anyone else?

She lifted her head to look at him, and found that he was looking back at her. His eyes were wide open. So were hers. And the silent message that passed between them let her know that for this moment, at least, he wasn't thinking of anyone else. She hoped he could see that she wasn't, either.

The song had barely ended when Spence took her hand and led her off the dance floor. He didn't pause at the table where they'd rested between numbers, but kept walking toward the exit. Libby followed without protest. She wanted to be alone with Spence.

She brushed someone's shoulder and murmured an apology, then realized belatedly that it was Don. He was looking at her with a rather startled expression, and Libby guessed that he'd watched her uncharacteristic behavior with Spence on the dance floor. She felt her cheeks warm and gave him a slight, rueful smile. He returned it with what might have been a touch of regret. Libby wondered if he was remembering that there had been a lot of laughter but little passion in their brief relationship. They had never kissed on a dance floor, never been so caught up in each other that everyone around them had faded to oblivion.

Libby hoped Don would soon discover that amazing sensation for himself, if he hadn't already. And she hoped even more fervently that this wouldn't be the last time she shared the experience with Spence.

SPENCE MEANT TO TAKE her straight home and leave her at her door. He really did. He said less than a dozen words during the drive home, taking that time to admonish himself to slow down, cool off, remember that he wasn't interested in getting tangled up with a woman—*any* woman—right now. And especially not this one, who was trouble if he'd ever seen it. Too many strings, too many expectations, too many awkward circumstances. No matter how great it had felt to hold her in his arms, it was time to back off. Time to call a halt before this went any further.

He thought he'd convinced himself. Thought he'd worked it all out. Until Libby turned to him at her door, gave him a smile that hit him like a punch in the stomach and lifted her face invitingly to his.

He kissed her because she seemed to expect him to. And then he kissed her because he wanted to. And then because he needed to. And then because he thought he'd die if he didn't.

He told himself he could stop even when they groped for the doorknob and tumbled into the entryway, their mouths still fused together. He told himself he would leave in just a minute, even as Libby pulled him toward the stairs and guided him up the steps with eager hands and frequent pauses for more wet, deep kisses. He reminded himself that he didn't want to get involved with her even as he fumbled to remove her clothing and his own, his burning impatience making him clumsy and awkward.

Somewhere between one long, drugging kiss and the next, sometime between his first taste of her breasts and the first tentative touch of her soft hand between his legs, he stopped fighting.

Tenderness. He found himself suddenly flooded with it, wanting to give and give and give, finding more pleasure than he could have imagined in her soft cries and ragged sighs. His hands slowed, his kisses lengthened, softened. With a generous patience he hadn't thought himself capable of, he took his time, lingering over every sweet inch of her until she was writhing helplessly beneath him on her bed.

And then he took her higher.

Libby provided protection from a drawer in her nightstand. She cried out his name when he thrust inside her. Spence couldn't speak at all. The pleasure was so intense, the feelings so very right, that he almost panicked and bolted from the room. But he found himself trapped by her soft arms and even softer hidden folds, and then he decided he didn't really want to run, after all.

Tenderness turned to passion, passion to raging hunger. Libby's nails dug into Spence's shoulders; his fingers dug into her thighs. The headboard thumped hollowly against the floral-papered wall; the aging bedsprings creaked in a timeless monotone. And when

Libby suddenly stiffened and cried out in release, Spence knew a savage satisfaction that was even more intense than the climax that hit him only seconds later.

It had been *his* name on her lips, he thought when he finally collapsed on top of her, both of them sweaty and trembling and gasping for air. Just as it had been Libby's name he'd groaned at that final, crucial moment. There had been only the two of them in the bed, thank God. For that all-too-brief time, the world—and the memories—had been held at bay.

But now his mind was clearing and the memories, the doubts and the recriminations were all pouring back in. He rested his head against Libby's and silently cursed himself for being such a fool.

LIBBY'S ALARM WOKE HER early Saturday; she had to go to the clinic that morning. She grumbled at being so rudely awakened and reached without opening her eyes to shut off the alarm. Only then did the memories of the night before return in painfully vivid color.

She groaned and buried her face in the pillow, wondering how long she'd been alone in the bed. She must have fallen asleep in Spence's arms, their damp bodies still intimately joined. Had he slept, too? Or had he slipped from the bed and left?

What in the world had happened? What had begun as a pleasant dinner and a little dancing had turned into an explosion of passion that had left her feeling bruised and shaken. She wasn't sure anything would ever be the same for her again.

She groaned again and pulled the pillow over her head.

She had fallen in love with Michael Spencer. What a monumentally stupid thing for her to have done.

9

LIBBY RAN TAP WATER into a glass and lifted it to her lips. She and Gran had just returned from church services and Gran, as always, had headed straight for the kitchen to finish preparations for the Sunday lunch that she'd begun at daybreak. Gran always made a big deal out of Sunday lunch, even for just the two of them. She often invited guests—the pastor and his wife, members of her Sunday school class, the deacon who'd lost his wife last year. Since she hadn't mentioned guests today, Libby assumed they were on their own.

Gran looked around from the oven. "I did mention that Jamie and Spence are joining us for lunch today, didn't I?" she asked, straightening her glasses with one flour-dusted finger.

The drinking glass slipped from Libby's hand and crashed against the bottom of the deep porcelain sink, breaking into three large pieces. "Damn," she said, dismayed at her clumsiness. "Look what I've done."

"Don't curse on the Lord's day, Elizabeth. It's not respectful," Gran chided.

"Sorry, Gran." Libby carefully tossed the broken glass into the trash container beneath the sink. "Mmm—no, you didn't mention that you'd invited the Spencers for lunch."

"You don't mind, do you?" Gran rarely checked with Libby before inviting guests, since she knew Libby never objected.

"Of course not," Libby lied blandly. "What can I do to help you get ready?"

She minded. She really, really minded.

She hadn't seen Spence since Friday night. She'd done an excellent job of avoiding him—or had it been Spence doing the avoiding? Whichever, she still didn't feel quite prepared to face him again. She had a terrible dread that he would take one look at her face and know that she was hopelessly, utterly in love with him. And then he'd probably run farther and faster than he had when he'd left her bed.

Had he been as shaken by what had passed between them as she had? Or did he regret the passion that had caught them both so unprepared, worrying now about embarrassing repercussions?

Oh, dear, how had she ended up in this mess? She, who'd always been so careful and organized and conscientious. She, who had always thought she knew exactly what she wanted and where she was going in her life.

"Libby?" Gran spoke in concern, her eyes searching Libby's face. "Are you all right?"

Heaven only knew how long she'd been standing there beside the sink like a freshly carved ice sculpture. She blinked and managed a smile, hoping it didn't look as sickly as it felt. "I'm sorry, Gran. I was just . . . thinking about something. What did you say I could do to help with lunch?"

STARING AT THE FRONT DOOR of Libby's house, Spence buffed the top of one boot against the back of his gray twill slacks and tugged at the left cuff of his dark blue shirt. He hadn't noticed until now that the cuff was a bit frayed. He wondered if there was time to run back to the cottage and change.

"Dad?" Jamie shifted impatiently beside him, scuffing her little black shoes against the walkway. "What are you waiting for? Gran said for us to be here at one and it's already two minutes after."

He'd stalled as long as he could. He would have made an excuse to turn down this invitation, but Jamie would have been terribly disappointed. Spence glanced down at his daughter. "Smooth your skirt, Jamie. Your hem is turned up again."

Jamie reached down to smooth the skirt of her deep purple velveteen dress with the white lace collar—her best dress. Spence noticed that the garment was getting a bit tight around her middle and a little short in the sleeves. She was growing almost faster than he could keep her in clothes. Before long she'd be a young woman.

He didn't even want to think about that.

Jamie touched a hand to the white bow Spence had painstakingly clipped to one side of her freshly washed, naturally wavy copper hair. "Do I look okay now?" she asked.

"You look beautiful," he said huskily, placing a proud hand on her shoulder. No man had ever had a more beautiful daughter.

The front door opened before Spence could ring the bell. "I thought I heard you out here," Gran said cheerily. "Come on in, lunch is ready. Jamie, you look so pretty!"

"Thank you," the child said with a broad, pleased smile. "I wanted to dress up and Dad said I could."

"I'm flattered that you went to so much trouble," Gran said, an amused twinkle in her eyes. She turned to Spence. "You look very nice, too, Spence. Had your ears lowered a bit, didn't you?"

"Yeah," Spence answered self-consciously. "I went to the barber yesterday."

"I went with him," Jamie announced. "They gave me bubble gum."

"How nice. Come on in now," Gran ordered, stepping back from the door. "Goodness, it's getting cooler, isn't it? It'll be winter before we know it."

"This week's Halloween," Jamie said, skipping through the door. "There's going to be a carnival at school. I'm going to dress up like a princess."

"A natural part for you," Gran assured her, smiling at Spence. "Libby's waiting in the dining room."

He wondered if she'd meant anything by that, then decided he was being an idiot. She had only been making conversation, for pete's sake. There was no need for him to start tensing every time he heard Libby's name. He was about to share another meal with her.

He tugged at the open collar of his shirt as though he were wearing a tie that had been knotted too tightly.

Libby was just placing a linen-covered breadbasket on the table when they joined her in the dining room. She glanced up, met Spence's eyes and dropped the basket with a soft thump. He wondered if she'd intended to set it down quite that hard.

She straightened and turned to Jamie, welcoming her with a smile and a compliment on her pretty dress. Spence noticed that Libby was looking very nice, too. He didn't often see her in a dress. The one she wore was a soft, green knit that molded nicely to her breasts, then flared into a full skirt around her shapely, stocking-clad knees. He couldn't help noticing the pulse beating in the tastefully scooped neckline. Was she as nervous as he was?

Was she furious with him for leaving without a word Friday night, for avoiding her so cravenly since? She certainly had every right to be.

He wasn't exactly proud of his behavior.

He couldn't explain exactly what had made him all but bolt from her bed, what had kept him figuratively on the run ever since. Nor could he understand why he couldn't think of their lovemaking without an underlying surge of panic. He'd tried to convince himself that he was overreacting, that it hadn't really been as special, as spectacular, as it had seemed. That he hadn't really responded to Libby in a way that he'd never responded to anyone—to *anyone*—before.

It had only been sex, he'd told himself ruthlessly. Nothing more. So there was no need to run scared. He certainly wasn't stupid enough to risk getting his heart involved with another woman who couldn't be more wrong for him. Especially since he still wasn't sure he was completely over the last woman who'd stolen his heart.

Libby turned finally away from Jamie and looked at Spence with a bland, distantly friendly smile that would have been perfectly appropriate for the mailman or the butcher. "Hello, Spence. I hope you're hungry. Gran's cooked enough to feed a small army."

"Yeah. I'm hungry," he growled, tempted to remind her that those coolly smiling lips hadn't been quite so cool when she'd pressed them to his . . .

"Let's all be seated, shall we?" Gran said brightly.

Mentally cursing himself, Spence held the back of a chair for the older woman.

She patted his cheek as she took her seat. "How gallant."

Spence flushed like a schoolboy, which only made him curse himself more viciously. This could quite possibly turn out to be the longest afternoon of his life.

He tried to keep his objectivity. Tried not to notice the little things about Libby that drove him crazy. Like the dimple that tucked her cheek when she smiled at Gran or Jamie—she certainly wasn't smiling much at *him* this afternoon. Or the way she licked her full lower lip after taking a sip of her iced tea. Or nibbled on a warm, buttered wheat roll with an almost sensual enjoyment that made him ache somewhere deep inside.

His objectivity didn't last through the salad Gran served before the main course.

He still wanted Libby. Wanted her so badly he could almost taste it. Damn it, he'd hoped he'd worked her out of his system Friday night. Now he was beginning to believe that heated interlude had only sharpened his appetite.

". . . don't you think, Spence?"

He brought his attention sharply back to the conversation flowing around him. "Sorry, Mrs. Grandjean. What did you say?"

"I said," she repeated patiently, "that we'd probably better be prepared for a hard frost soon. The weatherman says there's a good chance of freezing temperatures coming in the next week or so. The high tomorrow is only supposed to be in the fifties."

He was having a hard time concentrating on anything as mundane as the weather when his whole life was in an emotional turmoil. But he managed to nod and say politely enough, "I'll make sure the pipes and everything are protected from freezing. You'll need to let me know what you want me to do about your flower beds—I've never done much gardening."

The conversation centered on winterizing the property while they ate the main course of honey-baked ham and perfectly seasoned vegetables. Spence could have been eating sawdust, for all the notice he took of the meal his hostess had gone to such effort to prepare. He was busy trying to avoid Libby's all-too-perceptive eyes.

THEY WERE JUST finishing dessert—coconut pie—when Gran said, "Do you really have to go back to your clinic this afternoon, Libby? Can't you take even one full day off?"

Spence watched as Libby shook her head. "It's my turn to check on the animals," she explained. "I won't be too long. Unless something comes up, of course."

"Working yourself into an early grave," Gran muttered.

"Do you need any help checking on the animals, Libby?" Jamie asked eagerly. "I can help you feed them and water them and everything."

Spence was just about to tell Jamie not to bug Libby about going with her when Libby replied, "I don't see any reason why you can't go along, if it's okay with your dad."

Jamie turned instantly to her father. "Is it okay?"

Spence looked at Libby. "Wouldn't she be in your way?"

"No, of course not. I'm sure she'd be a lot of help."

"Okay, Dad?"

Spence looked at Jamie's hopeful little face and lifted one shoulder in a shrug. "Okay. Sure. Just do what Libby says and don't get into anything."

Jamie nodded avidly. "I'll be good, I promise. When are we going, Libby?'

"We'll both need to change clothes," Libby explained, smiling at the child's enthusiasm. "I'll help Gran clean up the kitchen first."

Spence suddenly noticed the expression in his daughter's eyes when she looked at Libby. Libby had become her heroine, he realized with a funny, hollow feeling in his chest. She was everything Jamie wanted to grow up to be.

It was the first time his kid had idolized anyone except him.

He glanced back at Libby, wondering what magic this fresh-faced, soft-voiced woman exerted that had Jamie—and him—so firmly under her spell.

"SO HERE YOU ARE."

Spence looked up from the saddle he'd been cleaning in the tack room of the barn. Libby stood in the doorway. "You looking for me?" he asked.

"Not anymore." She stepped into the small, neatly crowded room, brushing aside a hanging bridle that swung against her cheek when she walked beneath it.

Spence glanced at his watch. It was almost six, some three hours after Libby and Jamie had left for the clinic. "Just getting back?"

"Yes. I thought I'd let you know we're home, and tell you that Gran is making Jamie a ham sandwich for dinner. She said to tell you there are plenty of leftovers if you're hungry."

Spence shook his head. "After that huge lunch, it may be hours before I'm hungry again."

"I know how you feel." Libby ran a finger over a freshly polished bit as though looking for dirt or rust. Spence was confident she wouldn't find either.

"Did Jamie help you out or get in your way?" he asked to make conversation. It was too easy to think when it was quiet, too easy to notice all those inviting things about Libby that he was trying to ignore. Like the way her black-and-turquoise sweater clung to her small but perfect breasts. Or how nicely her washed-soft jeans fit her slender hips and thighs. There were a few dog and cat hairs clinging to her clothing. He was strongly tempted to brush each hair away with his fingers—and take his time about it.

"She helped," Libby replied, unaware that his thoughts had strayed into such dangerous territory since he'd asked the question. "She really is wonderful with the animals. And so eager to help. I'm crazy about that kid of yours, Spence."

"Yeah. Me, too."

The silence fell again, lying even more heavily between them this time. Spence looked up from the saddle and found Libby studying him through her lashes. Their gazes held.

"Did you—?"

"Have you—?"

They stopped.

Spence gestured with one hand for her to continue. She shook her head. "What were you going to say?" she asked.

"You first," he insisted.

She sighed. "I was just going to ask if you've been working any more with Tennessee. I've been gone so much lately, I've barely had time to pet him occasionally, much less put him through his new paces."

"Yeah. I've been working him. Jamie's been riding Alabama some, to keep her exercised. That's okay, isn't it?"

"Of course. She told me the two of you had been riding together. She enjoys it."

"Yeah. She does." He watched as Libby tucked a wayward curl behind her ear, and he remembered how sweet the soft skin just behind that pretty ear had tasted. His body stirred in reaction; he scowled.

Libby was watching him warily, as though wondering what she'd said to make him frown. He deliberately smoothed his expression.

"So, um, what were *you* going to say?" she prodded.

He might not have known that this awkward encounter was making her nervous if he hadn't noticed the way she twisted her fingers in front of her. It wasn't like Libby to be fidgety.

"I was going to ask if you'd mentioned to your grandmother that we had dinner together Friday," he said. He and Mrs. Grandjean had spent some time in the flower beds after Libby and Jamie left for the clinic that afternoon, but Mrs. Grandjean hadn't alluded to Friday night, and Spence hadn't wanted to bring it up. He wasn't sure what—if anything—Libby had told her Gran.

Libby's cheeks flamed, making Spence wonder if her mind had just flooded with some of the same images he'd been dealing with all afternoon. "No, uh, I forgot to mention it," she said.

He quirked an eyebrow. "You forgot?"

She tossed him a frown. "Okay, I just decided not to say anything. It—I—well, I just didn't know what to say."

He could understand that. "You okay?" he asked inanely.

"Of course I'm okay," she said, her chin lifting. "Why wouldn't I be?"

"Beats me," he muttered. So maybe he was the only one who'd been going crazy. Maybe it had just been a run-of-the-mill, Friday-night date for Libby. A little dinner, a little dancing . . . a little sex.

Like hell. There might be a lot of things he didn't understand about Libby Carter, but he knew her better than that. Which, of course, was part of the problem. He cleared his throat. "About Friday night—"

"What about it?" she asked cautiously.

"I hope you, uh, I just want you to know it, er . . ."

Libby crossed her arms in front of her and tilted her head to one side, studying him coolly. "Yes, Spence?"

Damn. He tossed the cleaning cloth he'd been using to the floor and pushed himself off the wobbly stool he'd been sitting on, stepping away from the saddle he'd draped over a padded sawhorse. "I just don't want you to get the wrong idea about what happened between us," he began firmly.

Libby startled him by smiling—a smile he didn't like at all. "Don't get all in a lather, Spence. I know exactly what happened between us."

"Yeah?" he asked suspiciously, planting his hands on his hips. "And just what is that?"

"Sex," she said succinctly, eerily echoing his earlier thought. "Proximity, hormones, curiosity—call it whatever you like. Anyway, it was a one-time thing, and if you're worried about me making more of it than that you can relax. I'm not asking for anything from you, Spence. You're perfectly safe from me."

He didn't like any of her descriptions for what they'd shared. He didn't like her implication that he was running scared of her. And no matter how contradictory he was acting, he found that he didn't at all like her casual declaration that it had been a "one-time thing."

"So you were curious about me, were you?" he asked, taking a small step closer to her. "About what it would be like between us."

She didn't quite meet his eyes. "Yeah. I guess I was. It's only natural."

"You're sure that's all it was? Just an itch we both needed scratched? Nothing serious? All worked out of our system now?" He moved closer as he spoke, slowly, so as not to spook her.

She was too busy twisting her fingers and staring at her purpling knuckles to pay much attention to what he was doing. "I wouldn't have put it quite so crudely, but, yes, I guess that's what it was. Basically."

He dropped his hands on her shoulders. "Liar."

Her startled gaze flew upward to his. "What—?"

"I'm not a temporary itch, Libby Carter, and what we shared wasn't a convenient scratch. I don't know what the hell it was, but it isn't out of my system. And I know damned well it isn't out of yours, either."

"But—"

There seemed to be only one way to make her face the facts. He closed his mouth over hers before she could sputter any more moronic arguments.

It had been maybe forty-three hours since he'd last kissed her. Yet he found himself kissing her as though he had weeks of abstinence to make up for—long, hungry, empty weeks. He'd memorized her every curve forty-three hours earlier. But now his hands raced over her as though to explore her all over again. He'd made love with her just forty-three hours ago. And yet his whole body shuddered with the need to bury himself inside her again.

No, it hadn't been a "one-time thing." One time—a hundred times—would never be enough with Libby.

What the hell was happening to him?

"Spence," Libby murmured, and the husky, breathless quality to her voice made him burn even hotter. "Oh, Spence—we shouldn't be doing this again."

He filled his right palm with the small, soft mound of her left breast. He could feel the hardened nipple even through her bra and sweater. He swallowed a groan. "No," he muttered. "We probably shouldn't. But, God, Libby, I want you again."

She arched into his touch, the movement seemingly an involuntary one. Her cheeks were flushed, her eyelids heavy. He felt the fine tremor that seemed to run through her and into him. Her movement brought her abdomen against his, the juncture of her thighs cradling the erection straining his already-tight jeans. He slid his left hand down her back to grasp her hip and drag her closer.

"Spence," she whispered once more. He thought she was going to tell him again to stop. Instead, she went up on tiptoes and wrapped an arm around his neck, crushing her mouth against his in a kiss that rocked him on his heels.

He groaned deep in his chest, hauling her so close against him that he worried about hurting her. If she was in pain, she hid it well. The soft sounds she made were whimpers of pleasure, and her hands were all over him. She slipped her tongue between his lips, mating it with his. The action sent him over the edge.

With one smooth effort, he pressed her against the wall, lifted her and wrapped her legs around his waist all at the same time. He kissed her mouth, her nose, her mouth, her cheek, her mouth, her ear, her mouth, her throat. Her mouth.

Libby returned the kisses frantically, her breath hot and fast in his ear, her legs squeezing him so tightly he could hardly breathe. He didn't care. It felt great. He slipped his hand beneath the hem of her sweater and upward, until his palm was filled with lace and warm flesh. He rubbed his thumb over the straining nipple. She shuddered and tangled her fingers in his hair. He shoved the sweater out of the way, lifted her higher, and tugged the lacy bra cup aside with his teeth. And then he was tasting her, tugging, suckling, gently biting, until her breath came in broken little pants and her legs tightened frantically around his waist. Only then did he move his hand between them, cupping her, feeling her moist warmth even through the denim of her jeans, longing to lose himself in that wet heat.

He was so hard, so full, so hot, he could have taken her right there, right then, not caring that they were standing up in a barn, that someone could walk in at any time, that he'd told himself this wouldn't— couldn't—happen again. "Libby," he muttered against her throat. "Libby. I want—"

"Libby? Dad?"

The child's call drifted in from outside, coming closer as she called again. Spence groaned a protest and leaned his forehead against Libby's, hearing her throaty gasp of dismay. She took several deep breaths, then pushed against his shoulders. "Let me down," she whispered. "I have to—"

He dropped her legs, then held her shoulders to steady her until she'd regained her balance. Ironic, he thought. He was shaking like a leaf, yet he was steadying her.

Libby swiftly straightened her clothes and then dragged both hands through her tousled curls. Her color was still high, her mouth still slightly swollen from his kisses, but her breathing was slowing, quieting. Spence breathed through his nose, sternly bringing his own riotous emotions under control. There wasn't much he could do about the condition of his body; he shoved a hand in his pocket, hoping to minimize the evidence of his unsatisfied arousal.

He stared at Libby, knowing his face was hard, set, his expression revealing little, if anything. "It wasn't a one-time thing," he couldn't resist telling her.

She wrapped her arms around herself again, looking suddenly fragile and defenseless. "How many times, Spence?" she asked. "How many times until you get tired of me? Until you leave?"

"I don't know," he admitted.

She flinched. "You really think I can just accept that? I'm no masochist. I don't want you to hurt me."

He couldn't think of an answer to that, didn't have time, anyway. Jamie appeared in the doorway, looking curiously from him to Libby. "There you guys are. Is something wrong?"

Libby turned to the child with a visibly strained smile. "No, nothing's wrong, sweetie. Your father and I were just talking. Did you finish your dinner?"

"Yes. It was good. But I came to tell you that you have a telephone call. Gran's holding the phone until you come in."

Spence couldn't resist commenting. "Another emergency?"

Libby shot him a quick glance. "Probably."

"I'm beginning to agree with your grandmother. You *are* going to work yourself into an early grave."

She pushed a hand through her hair again—he noticed that it still wasn't quite steady—and turned her back to him. "I guess that's my problem, isn't it?" she asked over her shoulder. And then she walked away from him, her head held high.

He was hurting her. And he hated himself for it. She deserved better than him. A whole hell of a lot better.

THE LAST WEEK of October faded into the first week of November. Libby could hardly have said when one day ended and the next began. She had thrown herself into her work with a vengeance that made her former dedication look like playing around. Her grandmother had lectured her; her partner tried to convince her to take time off, to let him take over for a while, even to escalate their search for another vet to ease their work load, but she couldn't seem to slow down. At least while she was working, there wasn't time to agonize over Spence and the inevitable heartbreak he would inflict on her.

She saw Spence occasionally, of course. Even with all the hours she spent away from home, it was impossible to avoid seeing him, if only in passing. And then Gran invited Spence and Jamie to join them for Thanksgiving dinner. It was probably the longest day Libby had ever spent. She and Spence smiled, talked, moved like robots through the afternoon—and might as well have been in different states.

She thought she'd made her feelings clear enough to him. She wanted him. She could be badly hurt by him. He had to know she cared about him. And he'd made his feelings plain, as well. He wanted her. But he wasn't promising not to hurt her. No matter how busy she'd been, he knew where to find her if he wanted to make any promises or offer any hope.

He hadn't made any effort to contact her.

There were times she wished she could accept what he *had* offered. Passion. Pleasure. An occasional stolen evening or glorious hour. But she knew herself too well. She loved him. She didn't want an affair with him. She wanted a real relationship. A commitment. At least a strong chance that he could learn to return her feelings.

He offered nothing.

Libby hated his ex-wife. She didn't know her, of course, didn't even know the whole story of what had happened between them. But she knew that the woman had made no effort to contact her beautiful daughter. And she knew that Spence had been terribly, painfully hurt. Disillusioned. So gravely wounded that he had no intention of opening himself up to Libby—maybe not to anyone—again. He loved only two things now—his daughter and his freedom, in that order.

He didn't love her.

And so she worked, looking for love in the fuzzy faces of the animals entrusted to her care, bolstering her badly bruised ego with the respect and success she found in her job. She saved her tears for the long, lonely nights when she lay alone in the bed in which she had, on one very special occasion, found a joy she had never experienced before and probably would never know again.

It was on the day after Thanksgiving when her body and her stamina finally gave out, overwhelmed by the demands she'd made of them. She didn't know exactly what happened. One minute she was standing in her office, discussing a perplexing canine infection with Paul. The next minute she was on the floor, her head spinning, her vision clouded, the sounds of her partner's worried exclamations echoing hollowly in her ears.

"That's it," Paul said furiously, helping her to a chair over her feeble protests that she was perfectly all right, that it had only been a momentary dizzy spell. "Whether you want to or not, you're taking a vacation, partner. And you aren't stepping foot back into this clinic until you've gotten some rest, is that clear?"

"But I can't take a vacation now," Libby argued, holding a trembling hand to her still-swimming head. "I have patients. Appointments. Commitments."

"You have a responsibility to yourself," Paul answered flatly. "And you haven't been honoring it. I can handle things around here for a few days. And whatever I can't do, I'm going to turn over to Steve Ledbetter."

"Steve Ledbetter?" Libby repeated, wondering if she were still having trouble thinking clearly. "The new vet school graduate who applied for a job a couple of weeks ago?"

"That's the one. You liked him. I liked him. We're hiring him."

"But he has no experience. He's just a kid."

"So were you when we started this operation," Paul reminded her ruthlessly. "He's eager and he's hungry, and most important of all, he's available to begin immediately. I'm calling him, Libby. You go home. Can you drive, or should I call someone to come after you?"

"Of course I can drive! But, Paul, I really think—"

He was rummaging in her desk. He pulled out her purse and her car keys and pressed both into her hands. "Go home, Libby Carter, or I swear I'm calling your grandmother. You've got ten minutes to clear out."

"Look, Paul."

"Nine and a half." He placed his hand on the telephone on her desk, keeping one eye on his watch.

"You can't—"

"Nine." He lifted the receiver.

Oh, Lord, he couldn't call her grandmother and tell her Libby had fainted. Gran would go nuts. "Paul, please."

"Eight and a half."

She shoved herself angrily out of the chair. "All right, damn it! I'm leaving. How long do you want me to stay away before you'll allow me to return?"

"A week should make a good start. Two, if you need them." He smiled and brushed a chaste kiss across her temper-flushed cheek. "Stop fighting it, Libby. You're officially on vacation as of now. Have a good time, okay?"

There didn't seem to be much she could do about it. Libby gave him a withering look, blinked back a film of miserable tears and turned on one heel to stalk out of the office.

It looked as though she was taking a vacation.

She wondered how she was supposed to avoid Spence now.

10

LIBBY SOON LEARNED, to her chagrin, that avoiding Spence for the next few days would be impossible. It seemed they were going to be vacationing together.

Strapped into the front passenger seat of her Explorer, she glanced at him sitting behind the wheel and wondered how she'd ended up heading for Branson, Missouri, with Spence, Jamie and Gran while a neighbor looked after their place. Jamie chattered happily to Gran in the back seat, just as though this trip had been planned for months instead of thrown together at the last moment.

Or *had* it been thrown together? Libby couldn't help wondering if Gran had been planning this for much longer than she let on. Libby hadn't forgotten Gran's frequent hints about her friend who owned the bed-and-breakfast in Branson, and the invitation for Gran and Libby to spend a few days there this first week of December. Libby would have almost bet that Gran would have found some way to get Libby to go with her even if she hadn't conveniently given in to exhaustion at work.

It was hard to read Spence's expression. Libby knew very well that he had been pressured into coming along as thoroughly as she had. Gran had probably given him some pathetic spiel about Libby's poor health and des-

perate need of a vacation, thrown in a little manipu-
lation for Jamie's sake—what child wouldn't enjoy
taking three days out of school for a trip to Branson to
see the Christmas displays and visit Silver Dollar City?
And Gran had insisted that all Spence and Jamie's ex-
penses would be paid since he would be doing all the
driving and "baggage toting." Libby knew Spence had
tried to get out of it. But he was here. Obviously he was
no more immune to Emma Grandjean's relentless ma-
nipulation than anyone else!

Libby slept some during the early-morning, three-
hour drive. She'd been sleeping quite a bit since Paul
had sent her home from the clinic four days ago. Obviously she had allowed herself to become more exhausted than she'd realized. The excited chatter from
Jamie and Gran more than made up for the self-
conscious silence from Libby and Spence.

It was a pretty drive. Two-lane highway mostly,
winding through rolling hills and high rock bluffs,
whole miles of countryside decorated with nothing
more civilized than trees and pastures and cows and
old, ramshackle barns. They passed through tiny
towns—Greenbrier, Clinton, Leslie, Marshall, St. Joe,
Pindall—some little more than a couple of churches,
service stations and craft shops. Yet even in this rural
area, progress had crept in. She saw a computer repair
shop sitting next to a tiny grocery, an old brick phar-
macy that advertised the latest videos for rent, a BMW
sitting beside a battered pickup at a busy diner. High-
tech country, she thought with a faint smile.

"Dad, could I have another cookie, please?" Jamie asked, already digging in the bag of snacks Gran had provided for the trip.

Spence looked wryly in the rearview mirror. "You're hungry again?"

"Not really," Jamie answered, making a face. "My mouth is just bored."

Libby swallowed a laugh.

Spence snorted. "Don't know how your mouth could be bored," he drawled. "You haven't stopped working it since we left Little Rock."

Jamie only giggled.

"One more cookie," Spence said. "But that's it, okay? We'll have lunch in Branson."

"Are we almost there?"

Spence glanced at Libby.

"It's not much farther," she answered. "We're almost to Harrison now. After that, it's just a few miles to the Missouri border—maybe half an hour from Branson, at the most."

"Hey, cool. What's that?" Jamie asked, pressing her nose to the window beside her.

"That's the Little Bell Wedding Chapel," Gran answered, following the child's gaze. "Isn't it sweet? A lot of couples elope to be married here."

"Where the heck *are* we?" Spence asked, speaking just a bit too loudly.

Libby couldn't help wondering if even the sight of a wedding chapel made him so jumpy. She answered calmly. "Bellefonte, Arkansas. Population three hundred and sixty-three," she added, reading a road sign.

"Libby's grandfather and I were married in a little chapel much like that one," Gran said with a reminiscent sigh. "It was during the war, and he was about to be shipped overseas. It was so romantic."

"Why don't we listen to some music?" Spence suggested, snapping on the radio. He punched the tuner button. "What do you want to hear—rock, country, easy listening?"

"I like country," Gran piped in immediately. "I can't wait to find out what shows Sylvia has arranged for us to see. Almost all the theaters have Christmas shows going on now, you know—Shoji Tabuchi, Mel Tillis, Wayne Newton, Andy Williams, the Osmond family, the Presleys. And Sylvia says lots of big names have been performing at the Grand Palace. She really had to pull some strings to get tickets for us."

"I'm looking forward to Silver Dollar City," Jamie said eagerly. "Do you think any of the rides will be working, even though it's winter?"

"Some of them will be," Gran assured her. "And there are quite a few cute shows to see there, and a huge children's area. Not to mention the decorations and Christmas lights. The Christmas season begins in early November and runs through Christmas Day, and the whole area goes all out. My Sunday school class went last year and there were miles and miles of lights everywhere. It was gorgeous. I can't wait for you to see it, Jamie."

Libby listened with only part of her attention as Gran and Jamie went on and on about their plans for the next four days. A Vince Gill hit was playing on the radio; Spence appeared to be listening to it, though Libby was aware that he looked at her occasionally with an expression she couldn't have begun to read. She was so intensely aware of him, sitting so close to her in the vehicle—his thigh muscles rippling as he worked the accelerator and brake, his large, strong hands loosely gripping the steering wheel. She stared at those hands, remembering . . .

A new song began, a recent release by one of Nashville's most popular female singers. Her throaty voice poured through the speakers, vibrating with the emotion of the lyrics.

Spence reached out suddenly and snapped the radio off with a bit more force than necessary. A heavy silence fell over the interior of the car. Even Jamie had grown quiet, her little face sober as she stared out the window.

"Why did you do that, Spence?" Gran asked curiously. "Don't you like Delilah Payton? She's one of my favorite singers."

"Sorry, Mrs. Grandjean. We're coming up on a big intersection and I don't know which way to turn. I'll need you or Libby to give me directions and I wasn't sure I could hear you with the radio on."

Gran seemed satisfied with the explanation. Libby wasn't. There was more to his reaction to that sad song than he'd admitted. She wondered if it reminded him of . . . anyone. "You'll turn right at the intersection, Spence," she said.

He nodded. Both he and Jamie were very quiet for a while. Jamie perked up again when they crossed the Missouri line and Gran informed her that they were getting very close to Branson. Spence didn't look as though he cared one way or another. For all the expression he showed, he could have been no more than a paid chauffeur for the trip.

Thoroughly exasperated with him, Libby asked herself for the dozenth time that day why she'd fallen in love with this moody, uncommunicative, unpredictable man. She had no answer, of course. She only knew that she did love him, despite everything.

She felt like such a fool.

THE TOURIST MECCA of Branson, Missouri, went all out for the holiday season. Everywhere they looked they saw the big green-red-and-gold wreath symbol pierced with the logo Ozark Mountain Christmas. The trademark sign hung on nearly every establishment and signpost in the city, letting tourists know which businesses were still open for the season.

"Which way do I turn?" Spence asked as they came to the intersection of Highways 65 and 76, at the exit he'd already been instructed to take.

"Turn left on 76," Libby answered. "Right would take us to old downtown Branson, which you'll certainly want to see while you're here."

"And be prepared, Spence," Gran said from the back seat. "Highway 76 tends to be a bit . . . crowded."

"Crowded" wasn't exactly the word. "Bumper-to-bumper" was a more accurate description of the traffic through the heart of Branson's tourist industry. Cars displaying licenses from every state and Canada inched down the road, along with dozens of tour buses, trolley buses, unusual-looking half-boat, half-bus vehi-

cles called "ducks" and a few hardy souls braving the
cool temperatures on Harley-Davidsons.

Jamie pressed her face to the window, gaping at the
sights. Even Spence seemed a bit startled by the number of souvenir and craft shops, motels, restaurants,
theaters, minigolf courses, bumper boat rides, go-cart
tracks and arcades—even a bungee-jumping tower—
crowded onto the five-mile stretch of road. Libby and
Gran had been regular visitors to Branson since Libby
was just a little girl, so they weren't surprised by the
scope of the operation, but even Libby was startled at
how many new buildings had gone up since the last time
she'd been there, only two summers earlier.

"I heard that Branson now has more beds than Las
Vegas," Gran announced, as proud as if she'd personally developed the area. "Why, it wasn't even thirty
years ago that this strip held only a few businesses and
a couple of family music shows. Silver Dollar City was
only a tiny crafts village built over Marvel Cave. Now
it's a huge operation, with over a thousand employees.
And I've lost count of how many theaters have opened
in the area. It's amazing that a city of less than four
thousand permanent residents can handle over a million and a half visitors a year."

Spence shook his head. "I have to admit this is different from what I expected." He looked at a huge sign
bearing Andy Williams's likeness. "Don't think I've
ever seen so many theaters and motels crowded into
such a small area."

Libby laughed. "No one's ever quite prepared for
Branson. You have to see it to believe it."

They stopped for lunch at a restaurant Gran recommended, then drove straight to Sylvia's Bed-and-Breakfast Inn. They were welcomed by Gran's long-time friend Sylvia Hatcher, a rotund, motherly woman who ushered them into her restored Victorian home with cheery enthusiasm and a breathless list of all the activities she had planned for them during the next four days.

"Just wait until y'all see the lights," she enthused. "It all lights up 'bout dark and you never saw anything prettier in your life. Nearly every town from Kimberling City to Springfield has its own display. Really gets you in the spirit of the holidays."

Libby reflected wryly that such an ostentatious celebration of the season was a bit too commercial for her tastes, but she kept the thought to herself. Sylvia was much too proud of her town's tourist-attracting holiday brainstorm to be open to any criticism of the monetary implications.

Sylvia had reserved the entire place for her friends—making four bedrooms available for her guests. Gran and Jamie selected cozy matching rooms that shared a bathroom between them. "It'll be just like a slumber party," Jamie said with a giggle.

That left the two bedrooms on the other end of the hall for Libby and Spence. They also shared a bath, though it wasn't connected to either room, but located about halfway down the hall. Libby suggested that it might be better if Spence and Jamie took two of the closer bedrooms; Jamie looked a bit offended by the implication that she needed her father to look after her. Gran shook her head, saying she and Jamie were looking forward to several late-night gossip sessions and she didn't want Libby "messing around with their plans."

Libby eyed her grandmother suspiciously, wondering if Gran was indulging in a spot of matchmaking by insisting that Libby and Spence should be sleeping so close to each other, so far from the others. But Gran met her eyes in perfect innocence, and Libby had to concede or risk embarrassing herself by making a big deal out of what should have been a minor incident.

Libby's bedroom was charming, tastefully decorated in yellow and white with glossy dark woods and delicate accoutrements. She could hear Spence moving around on the other side of the adjoining wall. Was his room as nice? Would he be as painfully aware of her sleeping so close as she would be of him?

A tiny desk in one corner of her bedroom held neat stacks of tourist pamphlets for Sylvia's guests. Libby ruffled through them, pausing to read a history of the area, beginning in the early 1900s when the author Harold Bell Wright had written *The Shepherd of the Hills*, a book about his experiences with the rugged, eccentric mountain people he'd discovered in the Ozarks. Marvel Cave had been attracting tourists regularly since the forties, and Silver Dollar City—originally conceived as a recreation of an 1880s Ozark Mountain village complete with demonstrations of mountain arts and crafts—had opened in 1960.

Also in the sixties, two local musical families had opened country-music-and-good-clean-comedy theaters on Highway 76, predating the more than thirty theaters now open to area visitors. And while the locals appreciated the wealth and prestige the surge of popularity brought into the area, they still struggled to preserve the natural, undeveloped beauty of the surrounding area—the wooded mountains, the fish-filled lakes and streams, the untouched hollows.

Libby enjoyed the frantic fun of the new Branson, but she couldn't help nostalgically thinking back to the days when her grandparents brought her when she was just a little girl and the area had been less crowded, much less commercial. She'd heard others express much the same regret now that their well-kept secret vacation spot for so many years had become internationally famous.

"I just read that history in my room," Spence said from the doorway. "Interesting."

Libby had left the door open, but she still jumped in response to his voice. She dropped the pamphlet and spun to face him. "Is, uh, is your room comfortable?" she asked.

"Yeah, it's fine. Your grandmother sent me to tell you that you've got about fifteen minutes to freshen up and meet everyone downstairs. We're going sight-seeing and then we have tickets to a show that begins at six. She says we have to get an early start because of the heavy traffic before the shows."

Libby smiled. "Gran's going to keep us very busy on this 'restful' trip."

Spence didn't return the smile. His dark eyes searched her face. "Are you up to this? Wouldn't it be better for you to take it easy for a few days?"

Libby shook her head. "I've been resting for the past three days. This is exactly what I need now—a good time away from the clinic."

"You'll say something if you get too tired?" he persisted. "I don't want you passing out again."

Libby felt her eyes widen. "How did you . . .?" She'd been so careful not to mention that particular incident to anyone, not wanting to worry her grandmother.

"Your partner called and told me when he found out that I'd be doing the driving on this trip," Spence admitted. "You scared the hell out of him. I knew something had happened, or you wouldn't have suddenly decided to take a vacation. You know it was incredibly stupid of you to work yourself to that point of exhaustion."

Libby flushed. "I didn't ask your opinion of my working habits."

He nodded coolly. "I'm aware of that. If you had, I'd have told you a lot sooner. You've got to start taking care of yourself, Libby, before you do permanent damage."

Her pride stinging, she lifted her chin. "Great advice from someone who regularly puts himself in splints and bandages chasing a rodeo buckle."

The barb hit home. His eyes narrowed. "That's my business."

"Right. And my health is mine."

"Fine."

"Fine."

"Fifteen minutes," Spence said again, reaching to close her door. "We'll be waiting downstairs."

"Fine."

He didn't respond this time, except to close the door with a peevish snap.

IF JAMIE OR GRAN noticed the tension between Spence and Libby that afternoon and evening, neither mentioned it. Jamie seemed to have a wonderful time exploring the area and then later watching the Presleys' Christmas show, laughing at the antics of the comics Herkimer and Harley Worthit, enjoying the mixture of country, gospel and traditional Christmas music. Libby enjoyed watching Jamie as much as she did the performances on stage. She'd forgotten how much fun it could be to view the world through the bedazzled eyes of a child.

It was late when they finally turned in. Libby was tired, but it took her a while to get to sleep. As she'd predicted, she was all too aware of Spence lying so close to her—yet so darned far away, both physically and emotionally. From the tossing and turning sounds coming from the room next door, she suspected he was having his own problems sleeping. She could only hope that she was bothering him as badly as he was bothering her.

GRAN OPTED OUT of the trip to Silver Dollar City the next day, leaving that to "the younger crowd." She wanted to stay behind and visit with her friend in the cozy warmth of the inn. It was left to Libby, Spence and Jamie to brave the cool temperatures and milling crowds at the theme park.

Jamie oohed and aahed over the lavish Christmas decorations in the park, making it look like an authentic turn-of-the-century town dressed up for the holidays. Captivated by Jamie's delight, Libby and Spence put aside their personal problems and made sure that

Jamie had a wonderful time. Together they visited the crafts shops, toured the awe-inspiring caverns, crossed swinging bridges and strolled down wooded pathways.

They drank root beer and ate peanuts while watching a performance in the saloon, sipped hot cider to warm themselves when the afternoon got cooler, munched on roasted corn on the cob, grilled chicken, freshly made fudge and hot, sugar-dusted funnel cakes. They visited Santa Claus, talked to roving entertainers dressed in period costumes, listened to music from dulcimers, banjos and Autoharps, staggered laughingly through the crazy-gravity fun house called Grandpa's Mansion, then tiptoed reverently through the authentic Wilderness Church, with its glass wall looking out over miles and miles of untamed mountain beauty.

And when the sun set and the thousands and thousands of tiny white lights strung around the park were turned on, even Spence had to admit that the park looked like a Christmas fantasyland. Jamie was thrilled speechless almost.

"This is the best place in the whole world," she declared, one little mittened hand nestled snugly in Spence's hand, the other in Libby's, as she skipped along between them.

Libby smiled around the sudden lump in her throat. "I'm happy that you're enjoying it, Jamie."

The child smiled happily up at her, her eyes glowing beneath the hood of her down-filled blue coat. "I am. I'm glad we came, Libby. We're just like a real family, aren't we?"

Libby caught her breath. Her gaze clashed with Spence's over Jamie's head. His expression was faintly startled, his cheeks reddened from the cool air—and something else?

"I hear the train whistle, Jamie," he said rather abruptly. "We'd better hurry to the train station. The guy at the blacksmith shop told me the train runs through the woods and that Christmas light displays have been set up all along the path. He said we don't want to miss it."

"After we ride the train, can I go see Santa again, Dad?" Jamie asked suddenly. "I just thought of something else I want to ask for for Christmas."

"What's that, punkin?" Spence asked, leading her through the crowds toward the train station.

Jamie looked slyly from her father to Libby and then back again. "It's a secret," she said gravely.

Spence lifted an eyebrow. "You'd better let me in on it if you want to make sure you get it," he advised.

But Jamie only smiled and tightened her grip on their hands, keeping them close together. Looking, Libby thought wistfully, very much like a family.

JAMIE WAS SOUND ASLEEP by the time they returned to the inn late that evening. Spence carried her inside. Libby helped him dress the child in her pajamas and tuck her into bed.

Libby couldn't resist leaning over Jamie's bed to kiss the child's soft little cheek before leaving the room. Jamie's eyelids fluttered and she smiled. "'Night, Libby."

"Good night, sweetheart." Libby realized only then that she had fallen as completely in love with Spence's

child as she had with the man himself. It was a rather
staggering revelation. She wanted to be a part of this
family, wanted it so badly she could almost taste it. It
hurt to want that badly. She let herself out of the room
while Spence leaned over the bed to deliver his own
good-night kiss to his daughter.

Gran and Sylvia had already turned in, having left a
note for Libby and Spence urging them to help themselves to a late-night snack if they wanted and saying
they'd meet them for breakfast the next morning in the
dining room. The big house was very quiet, giving
Libby the illusion that she and Spence were alone as
they stood in the hallway outside Jamie's door.

"Do you want some hot chocolate or something?" she
whispered.

He shook his head. "I've had so much to eat and
drink today that I couldn't handle another drop."

"Same here," she admitted. She'd made the sugges-
tion only because she wasn't quite ready to tell Spence
good-night.

"Guess we'd better turn in," Spence said, shoving his
hands into his jeans pockets. "Your grandmother probably has a full day planned for us again tomorrow."

"Probably," Libby conceded. It seemed that Spence
didn't share her desire to spend more time together.
Maybe, she thought regretfully, he'd had his fill of her
today.

"Good night."

She turned toward her room. "Good night."

She half hoped he'd stop her. That he would at least
want to kiss her after they'd shared such a lovely day
together with Jamie. He didn't say anything as she

stepped into her room and closed the door reluctantly behind her.

Libby drifted restlessly to the window to stare out at the star-studded night. It was cool by the window; she shivered and wrapped her arms around herself, snuggling more deeply into the hand-knitted cotton sweater she'd worn with jeans that day. She felt very much alone.

The door opened quietly, without warning.

Spence still wore his shirt, jeans and boots, though he'd discarded the pullover sweater he'd had on earlier. His hair was tousled, his jaw shadowed by an evening's growth of beard. His eyes were dark, turbulent, his mouth set in an unsmiling line.

Libby swallowed hard. "Was there—is there something you want, Spence?"

"Yes." He stepped into the room and silently closed the door behind him. "I want you."

She caught her breath. She wanted so badly to ask how long he would want her—was it only for tonight or was he, too, beginning to picture them as a family? But the question froze on her lips. She was afraid to ask it, afraid she wouldn't want to hear the answer.

"Libby?" he said when she stood silently staring at him. He moved closer, not touching her, but never taking his gaze away from hers. "If you want me to go, just say so."

"No," she whispered. "I don't want you to go." *Not tonight. Not ever.*

He lifted a hand to her face, cradling her cheek in his palm. She covered his hand with her own. "I tried to stay away from you," he muttered, his hungry eyes devouring her face. "I tried to tell myself it was better—for you, for both of us."

She turned her face to press a kiss into his palm. "You were wrong."

"I don't know. Maybe."

"You were wrong," she repeated firmly. "It isn't better when you stay away from me. It hurts too badly."

His other hand rose, slowly, so that her face was framed between them, her mouth only inches from his. "You give too much, Libby. You hurt too easily."

"I'm not the only one who hurts." She slid her hand up his chest, letting it rest just above his heart. "She hurt you," she said, not bothering to clarify who she meant. There was no need; they both knew she referred to his ex-wife. "And now you're afraid to let me close enough to take away the pain."

Spence frowned. "I don't want to talk about her."

"I know you don't. But not talking about it doesn't make it hurt any less, does it?"

He made a muffled sound that could have meant anything, then lowered his head to kiss her. Had he been unable to resist any longer—or was he only trying to stop the words that made him so uncomfortable? Whatever his reason, Libby cooperated wholeheartedly, rising on tiptoes to slide her arms around his neck and deepen the embrace.

She knew he wasn't hers yet, knew he was being torn between the hurts of the past and the needs of the present. And while she didn't want to believe that all she was to him was a convenience, a way of forgetting his pain for a few passionate hours, she couldn't resist reaching out to him. Wanting to hold him, to ease his lonely suffering. Loving him.

She twined her fingers in his hair and returned the kisses with a fiery voracity that more than matched his. Sometime during the day they'd spent together—maybe sometime during the past five minutes—she'd come to a decision. She was in love with this man. And it was time to start fighting for him. Whatever it took to banish his ex-wife from his heart, from his memories, she'd do it. She was fighting for herself, for Jamie, for Spence. They needed each other, damn it.

They made love silently, urgently. Clothing fell in haphazard piles on the floor; avid mouths and clever hands raced across taut, sweating skin. They rolled across the bed, racing toward the ecstatic release they'd found together only once before. She would have cried out when her powerful orgasm hit her; he managed to retain enough discretion to muffle her mouth with his own. His smothered groan signaled his own climax.

Awash in sensual pleasure, Libby smiled into his throat. She considered that first battle a victory for her side.

11

THEY LAY IN A DAMP, panting tangle for a long time afterward, until Spence noticed that Libby was beginning to shiver. "You need to be under the covers," he murmured, lifting her away from him so that he could reach for the sheets and blanket they'd shoved to the foot of the bed. "And I'd better get back to my own room. Wouldn't want Jamie or your grandmother to catch us in bed together in the morning."

"No. But stay a little longer. Please."

She could see that he didn't really want to leave yet. She was relieved when he hesitated only a moment before nodding and pulling the covers over both of them. "C'mere," he said.

Still shivering, she snuggled against him. "Keep me warm."

His smile was wicked when he wrapped an arm around her bare back. "I thought I had been."

She loved it when he smiled that way. He did it too rarely. She nestled into his shoulder and pressed a kiss to his cheek. "That's quite a healthy ego you've got there, cowboy."

He chuckled. "You're damned good for this cowboy's ego, lady."

"I'm damned good for this *cowboy*," Libby corrected him boldly. "He's just too stubborn to admit it."

To her regret, Spence's smile dimmed and his eyes shadowed. After a moment of silence, he said, "I'm a lousy risk for a relationship, Libby. You've probably already figured that out for yourself, I guess."

"No."

"Then you should have. Trust me, I've got a rotten track record—with women, with family—hell, even with my own mother."

"Tell me about your mother." She held her breath, hoping he was finally in a mood to talk. Hoping she hadn't read him wrong. Hoping her questions wouldn't send him running for his own room again.

He hesitated just long enough to make her nervous before he finally sighed and spoke. "I don't think she ever quite understood me," he admitted. "She was raised in a family of women. Her father died early and her mother raised her and her three sisters alone. She was young when she married my dad, young when she had me. I was one of those kids who somehow managed to tumble into trouble all the time. She sometimes said she spent more time with me in the emergency room than she did at home. I was always breaking something or cutting myself or getting bumped and bruised."

"The adventurous type," Libby interjected quietly, smiling a little at the thought of a young, curious, accident-prone Spence.

"I guess so. There were always so many things to do and see, so many challenges to try. My dad was a construction worker, and he and his buddies got a kick out of my exploits. Mom accused him of egging me on. It put a strain between them, I think. She wanted to coddle me and keep me safe, he wanted to turn me into a 'real man' long before I was through being a boy. And then he died."

"And you kept trying to be a 'real man,'" Libby hazarded.

"Yeah." He sounded a bit surprised by her insight. "I guess I did. I didn't want to let Dad's memory down."

"And your mother didn't know how to reach you."

"No, I suppose she didn't," he said with a sigh. "Especially after she married Carl."

"What's Carl like?"

"Nice guy. Total opposite from my dad. Carl's an accountant. Quiet, careful, obsessively organized. He likes to listen to opera."

Libby bit her lip against a smile. The last sentence had pretty well summed up Spence's feelings about his stepfather. He couldn't identify with him at all.

"Anyway," Spence continued. "Mom and Carl had twin girls when I was fifteen. Mom had babies to fuss over again and to overprotect, and Carl was nutty about the girls. He was good to me, really, tried his best to find things in common with me, but it just didn't work out. It seemed easier for all of us when I found other things to occupy my time."

"Rodeo."

"Yeah. Rodeo."

Just the way he said the word told Libby so much. The rodeo had become his life, his family, the challenges he needed that he could no longer find at home.

"I hit the road the day after I graduated from high school," he said. "Never looked back, though I try to call Mom every now and then. Man, I had some great times in those early years. Didn't have much money, but I sure had some fun."

"And then you met Jamie's mother."

His reminiscent smile vanished. "Yeah."

Libby ran a finger through the light dusting of hair between his nipples. "You fell in love with her."

"Big time. It was a condition I'd managed to avoid before that," he said dryly.

"Was she involved in the rodeo, too?"

"Yes. She rode—and she sang. Every man who knew her was half in love with her."

It hurt, but Libby couldn't seem to stop asking the questions. She had to know what she was up against, had to know her enemy before she could win the fight. "Did she love you?"

Spence shrugged. His voice hardened. "She loved the way I loved her. She needed to be adored, needed to be idolized. And I was stupid enough to give her everything she wanted—until it wasn't enough for her any longer. Until she needed a hell of a lot more than I had to offer."

"Was there—" Libby had to stop to swallow. "Was there someone else?"

"Thousands of someone elses," Spence muttered cryptically.

She let it go. "How long were you married?"

"Six years. The last three were hell—her trying to get away, me trying to hold her back."

"Have you seen her since the divorce?"

"I haven't seen her since the day she walked out on me taking nothing with her but the clothes on her back. She left a note telling me to sell everything else and use the money to take care of Jamie. She told me she loved me, and loved our kid, but it wasn't enough. She needed more."

"She didn't love you, Spence," Libby said fiercely, lifting her head to stare at him through a film of unshed tears. "No woman who really loved you would walk away from you and Jamie that way. She would have stayed to work it out."

"She was miserable with me."

"Then she should have talked to you about it, let you help her find ways to make her happy without destroying your family."

Spence sighed and stared at the ceiling. "There are a lot of things about . . . about my ex-wife you still don't understand."

"Then tell me."

"No." He touched her cheek, fleetingly, apologetically. "Not tonight."

"All right," she said. He'd given so much more than she'd expected already; she would wait until he was ready to reveal the rest. "Just promise me one thing, Spence."

His expression turned wary. "I don't know if I can make any promises tonight, Libby. I don't want to hurt you, but—"

"I'm not asking for a lifelong vow," she interrupted firmly. "I only want you to promise me that you'll stop comparing me to her. That you'll give me a chance to show you I'm not like her."

She had to stop again, and the breath she took was for courage. "I love you, Spence. And I love Jamie. I want to make a real family with you, one in which you can be free to be yourself, to do what makes you happy. I have my own life, my own career, so I don't need an emotional crutch or an adoring male to give me a sense of self-worth. I want a mate, a partner, an equal. I want a husband, children, love that doesn't try to change me or manipulate me. I have that same healthy sort of love to offer in return."

He was so still, so silent.

She went on. "I know you aren't ready to make a commitment, that you haven't had time to find out if you want the same things I want. Just give me a chance, Spence. That's all I'm asking. Come spring, if you still want to go back to your footloose life on the road, I swear I won't do anything to hold you back. I won't make any scenes, won't deliberately hurt you or Jamie. Just give me a chance. Please," she ended, her voice breaking.

He pulled her against him so tightly that she could hardly breathe, his arms locked around her with bruising intensity. "Damn it, Libby," he groaned, his voice raw. "Don't beg—oh, God, can't you see I'm not worth that?"

"You are to me," she whispered, tears escaping to trickle down her cheeks and wet his shoulder. "You are to me."

He buried his face in her hair. She could feel the tremors running through him. He was fighting her, she realized—fighting himself, she hoped. He would soon learn that she would make a formidable opponent.

This was the most important challenge she'd ever faced—earning Michael Spencer's love and his trust.

He took her by surprise when he rolled to loom over her, his expression grave, his gaze locked with hers. "You are one hell of a woman, Libby Carter," he said. "Smart and capable and generous and loving. You're probably the best thing that ever happened to me. You sure as hell deserve a lot better than me."

She started to rebut him, when he continued. "I can't make any promises now. God knows I don't have much to offer, and I have no right to ask you to be patient with me. But I need time, Libby. Time to work some stuff out for myself before I can decide if I want to risk getting permanently involved with anyone again."

"You have all the time you need," she told him, her heart quivering with hope. "I told you, I'm not asking for promises yet. For now, it's enough just to be with you. To be a part of your life, and of Jamie's."

They both knew it wouldn't always be enough. That there would come a time when she'd need much more. But it was enough for now, and that was all she could ask.

Spence was looking worried again. "You deserve more," he repeated.

She smiled and lifted a finger to his lips. "Why don't you let me decide that for myself."

He lowered his head to kiss her. "I have to go," he murmured when he finally lifted his head.

"I know."

He kissed her again. "I have to go *now*." He didn't move.

She giggled. "I know."

He nuzzled her temple, her ear, her throat. "You aren't helping."

"I'm not holding you here," she challenged, though she clung to his warm, sleek shoulders.

He kissed her one last time, then groaned and shoved himself out of the bed. He paused to tuck the covers snugly around her throat—much as he had for Jamie earlier, Libby couldn't help noticing wryly. He stepped into his jeans, leaving them unsnapped, tossed his shirt over his shoulder and carried his boots and socks in one hand as he walked quietly across the room.

He turned with one hand on the doorknob. "Good night, Libby."

"Good night." And then she couldn't resist adding, "I love you, Spence."

"I—" He stopped, swallowed, then murmured, "Good night."

A moment later, he was gone.

Libby let out a long, shaky breath. She'd taken quite a risk tonight, admitting her feelings to Spence. But he hadn't bolted, hadn't rejected her love—exactly. He had just asked for time, which she was perfectly willing to give him as long as she had reason to believe there was hope for them. And the look in his eyes when he'd kissed her, when he'd tucked the covers so tenderly around her, when he'd reluctantly left her bed, gave her the hope she so desperately needed.

She'd taken the greatest risk of her life. Now she could only pray that it paid off. Losing Spence now would be so devastating that she wasn't sure she'd ever recover.

BREAKFAST WAS A CHEERY affair, with Jamie chattering excitedly about her day at the theme park and Gran and

Sylvia indulgently responding to the child's enthusiasm. Libby hadn't been sure what to expect from Spence—would he regret the confidences that had passed between them during the night? Would he now be worried about her confession of love? Would he try to pull back? She was delighted when he slid into the chair beside her, dug into his breakfast with a healthy appetite and slid one hand beneath the table to teasingly stroke her thigh while he chatted blandly with her grandmother.

"We're going shopping in the Grand Village this morning," Gran announced. "It's a lovely little center filled with specialty boutiques that carry some unique merchandise. Bundle up, though. The shops are built around an open cobblestone plaza. It'll be chilly."

Libby slanted a look at Spence from beneath her lashes to see how he reacted to the news that he'd be spending the morning shopping in "specialty boutiques." He looked good-naturedly resigned. She placed her hand over his on her thigh and gave him an encouraging squeeze, which he returned immediately.

Bundled into coats, hats and gloves, they left right after breakfast. Sylvia stood in the doorway and waved them off, loudly wishing them a nice day.

They'd all grown accustomed to the slow-moving traffic by now, so took it in stride. Jamie began to sing—a strange tune about "bigger, better booger burgers."

Spence gave her a look in the rearview mirror. "I think that's enough of that one."

She flashed back an exaggeratedly angelic smile. "All the kids at school sing it."

"Save it for school, then. If you've got to sing, try a Christmas carol."

She obligingly broke into a chorus of "Jingle Bells." Gran promptly joined in. Libby laughed and added her own voice to the trio. Libby and Gran were both startled when Spence started to sing along in a decent tenor.

Libby couldn't remember being so relaxed—or so happy—in a very long time.

Following directions Sylvia had given them, they took a back road to the Grand Village to avoid the worst of the traffic on 76, coming in from Green Mountain Drive at the back of the shopping center. As they turned into the parking lot, Gran pointed out the four-thousand-seat theater next door. "That's the Grand Palace," she explained. "It's where most of the big-name stars perform when they visit Branson. When we leave here, we'll drive around front so you can see the facade—it's beautiful. Looks like a huge antebellum mansion."

They spent more than two hours in the shopping village, shivering in the plaza, gratefully enjoying the heated shops, stopping for hot chocolate at the Hard Luck Diner. Jamie was almost giddy with the pleasure of being with her father, Libby and Gran. She was the center of attention, chattering, skipping, exclaiming over the merchandise that interested her. Libby had noticed the day before that the child never asked for anything, but was always touchingly pleased when Spence—or, even more often, Gran or Libby—couldn't resist buying something for her.

"You're going to spoil her," Spence warned with a hint of a frown when Libby bought Jamie a tiny stuffed monkey at a stuffed-animal boutique.

"I can't resist it," Libby whispered back. "She's so sweet." She patted Spence's cheek, knowing Jamie and Gran were too wrapped up in the shelves of goodies to notice. "Don't worry, Spence, I won't get carried away. It's just for this one perfect day, okay?"

He smiled. "I'll hold you to that."

"I know."

He took her hand. And then continued to hold it even when they left the store, when Gran and Jamie couldn't help but notice. Gran's eyebrows rose speculatively, but she kept her thoughts to herself, though she smiled in apparent satisfaction. Jamie took Libby's other hand, holding it tightly. And even as Libby smiled down at the child, she wondered why she suddenly found herself terrified that something was about to go wrong, that the day had been *too* nice, *too* perfect.

Chiding herself for being both superstitious and paranoid, she climbed into the Explorer with the others after stowing her purchases in the back. She rubbed her hands together and then touched the end of her chilled nose, laughingly admonishing Spence to hurry and turn on the vehicle's heater.

"Wouldn't it be great if it snowed?" Jamie asked from the back seat. "That would really make it look like Christmas."

"It doesn't snow much around here, punkin," Spence said.

"Oh, it usually snows here a couple of times a year," Gran corrected. "But maybe we'd better hope it doesn't on this trip, sweetie. Those winding mountain roads back home are hard enough to navigate without having snow to make them slippery."

Jamie sighed. "I don't want to go back home yet," she said. "I love it here with you guys."

Gran reached over to give the child a hug. "We have two more days here, darling. We'll make the most of them."

Spence turned left out of the Village, heading toward the main strip again. They rounded the front of the Grand Palace and Jamie exclaimed over the beauty of the white, gracefully columned facade, all dressed up in greenery and red ribbons for the season. "How pretty!" she cried.

"It is, isn't it?" Gran agreed. "And we've got tickets for the show tomorrow evening. Sylvia had to really pull some strings to get them—the show's been sold out for weeks."

"Who's performing?" Libby asked casually, not that it mattered. As long as she was with Spence and Jamie, she didn't particularly care who they saw.

"See for yourself," Gran said, pointing to the huge sign that had just become visible to them as they reached the intersection of Green Mountain Drive and Highway 76.

A much-larger-than-lifesize, full-color photograph smiled down at them from the sign. The woman's long red hair and brilliant blue eyes would have been immediately recognizable even had it not been for the brightly lit letters spelling out her name. Delilah Payton. Country music's reigning sweetheart.

The silence that fell in the vehicle was heavy enough to touch. Spence slammed on the brakes. Jamie stared with a stricken expression at the beautiful face on the sign.

Libby looked from Jamie to Spence, noticing in bewilderment that his expression had turned to unrevealing stone. "Spence?" she asked, staring at his rock-hard expression. "What is it?"

He pressed his foot on the accelerator, easing into the traffic without looking at the sign again. He didn't respond.

Gran was reaching out to Jamie. "Honey, what is it?" she asked, worried about the child's sudden silence and pale little face. "What's wrong?"

Spence glanced in the rearview mirror at his daughter. "You okay, kid?"

Jamie managed a weak smile. "Sure, Dad. I'm getting kind of hungry, though. Can we eat now?"

"You bet. What do you want? Chicken? Hamburger? Pizza?"

"Hamburger—if it's okay with everyone else," Jamie replied.

Libby was watching the child over the back of her seat. She studied Jamie's soft, copper hair and huge, haunted blue eyes and remembered the red-haired, blue-eyed woman pictured on the sign. Surely not . . . But then she remembered the things Spence had said about his ex-wife. *She rode—and she sang. Every man who knew her was half in love with her.*

Libby turned to Spence. He slanted her a look. "Yeah," he said quietly, in answer to the silent question in her eyes. "My ex."

Delilah Payton. Libby fell back against the seat and stared out the side window, no longer noticing the passing scenery. Oh, damn.

Jamie recovered more quickly than Libby or Spence. Gran, still not quite certain what had happened to shake them so badly, went all out to make Jamie smile again, and soon succeeded. Libby ate, talked and moved mechanically, her mind a jumble of questions, her chest aching. She couldn't begin to read Spence's expression.

She couldn't even begin to define her own emotions at the moment. She wasn't quite ready to examine them that closely.

THEY SAW ANOTHER SHOW that evening—Mel Tillis's Christmas performance, this time. Jamie and Gran seemed to enjoy it immensely. Libby knew she would have loved it herself had she not been hurting so badly. It was late when they returned to the inn. Jamie and Gran went straight to their rooms, after kissing everyone good-night. Libby escaped to her own room, unable to stand another minute of being with Spence and knowing that he was so far away from her emotionally. He had hardly looked at her all afternoon, hadn't touched her again. She wouldn't push him, would give him the time he needed, but the pain was almost more than she could bear.

She changed out of the black-and-gold sweater and black slacks she'd worn to the theater and dressed in a warm, brushed cotton gown that covered her from throat to feet. She brushed her short curls and stared somberly at her reflection. She couldn't help comparing the wholesome-looking, boyishly figured woman in the mirror to the voluptuous, ultrafeminine, nationally famous Delilah Payton. Libby had seen Delilah only in photographs and on television, but she'd always considered the singer to be a stunningly beautiful woman, the fantasy ideal of red-blooded men all over the country.

No wonder Spence hadn't been immediately taken by her own appearance, Libby thought dully. Not when he'd had his memories of Delilah to compare her to.

She set down her hairbrush and wondered how any woman could walk away from her family. It was hard enough to imagine any woman leaving Spence, but how could Delilah have left little Jamie behind? How could she have preferred the applause of strangers to being with her own child?

Libby lifted a hand to her temple, feeling the veins throbbing just below the skin. She would never be able to get to sleep, she thought. She couldn't even force herself to climb into bed. Every time she looked at the bed, she thought of Spence and wondered if their lovemaking had really been as special, as earth-shattering for him, as it had been for her. Had he and Delilah—?

But, no. She could drive herself crazy that way.

On a sudden impulse, she snatched up her chenille robe and belted it tightly around her. She would slip down to the kitchen. Have a cup of chocolate and a couple of aspirin. Maybe find something to read. Maybe watch a late-night movie. Anything to help her tune out her thoughts and perhaps relax enough to catch a few hours of sleep.

Some impulse made her stop outside Jamie's room. She thought she heard a sound coming from inside the darkened room and paused to listen. And then her heart clenched as she identified the sound.

Jamie was crying.

Libby tiptoed into the room, finding the huddled little figure in the bed. "Jamie? Sweetheart, it's okay. Don't cry."

Jamie caught her breath on a broken sob. And then she threw herself into Libby's arms.

Libby sat on the edge of the bed and caught the child against her, her lips pressed to soft copper curls. She stroked Jamie's back through her thin flannel gown, crooning and instinctively rocking her upper body. "It's okay, baby. It's all right," she murmured, her voice a soothing litany. "I'm here."

"Don't tell Dad," Jamie pleaded, tightening her arms around Libby's neck. "It'll make him feel bad if he finds out that I cried. You won't tell him, will you, Libby?"

"Not if you don't want me to," Libby assured her. "But your father would understand, Jamie. You know he loves you more than anything in the world, don't you? You know you can talk to him about anything that's bothering you."

"I know," Jamie whispered. "But he gets sad sometimes. I don't like it when he's sad."

"No," Libby murmured, her eyes closing on a brief spasm of pain. "Neither do I."

Jamie swiped at her wet cheeks with the back of one hand. "He hasn't been sad so much lately. Not since he met you."

Libby bit her lip, wondering how to respond.

Jamie didn't give her a chance to answer. "We don't need *her* anymore," she said fiercely. "She didn't want us, and we got along just fine without her. I never even tell anyone she's my mother—they probably wouldn't believe me, anyway."

Libby winced at the bitterness in the child's voice. Jamie was much too young to be harboring that much anger, that much resentment. "Oh, sweetie. It couldn't have been easy for your mother to leave you," she said, wishing she knew some magical words to say, feeling so inadequate. "She must have had some very strong reasons to take such a drastic step."

Jamie shrugged. "I guess it's not nearly as exciting to be stuck with a kid as it is to be a rich-and-famous singer."

A flicker of anger heated Libby's blood—anger at the selfish, self-centered woman who'd put that note in a child's voice. "Listen to me, Jamie. You are a fantastic kid. You're bright and funny and sweet and thoughtful and any woman would be thrilled to have a daughter like you. I don't ever want you to think there's anything lacking in you. Your mother may have gained fame and fortune when she left, but she gave up so much more. Someday she's going to realize that—and regret it."

Jamie looked searchingly at Libby's face. "Would you—would you be thrilled to have a daughter like me?" she asked in a small voice.

Libby's own voice broke. "Oh, sweetheart. I would give anything to have a daughter just like you. I can't think of anything that would make me prouder or happier."

Jamie buried her face in Libby's shoulder, her arms clinging tightly. "I wish you were my mother."

Libby swallowed what felt like an enormous lump in her throat. She kissed Jamie's forehead and hugged tightly. And then something made her look toward the doorway.

Spence was watching them with an expression that tore Libby's heart. How long had he been there? How much had he heard?

He held her gaze for a long, taut moment, then turned and slipped away without a sound.

Libby stayed with Jamie awhile longer, until the child's eyelids were drooping heavily. And then she tucked her back into bed. "You don't have to go to that concert tomorrow, Jamie," she promised. "We'll find something else to do. Something fun."

"No," Jamie murmured, snuggling into the pillow. "I think I want to go. If Dad does, of course. You'll go with us, won't you, Libby?"

"We'll see." Libby had no intention of making promises she might not be able to keep.

Jamie didn't argue. She was asleep before Libby left the room.

Libby paused outside Jamie's door to make sure the child was really asleep. And then she took a deep breath, tucked a wayward curl behind her ears and headed toward Spence's room.

Something told her that Spence needed her now as badly as Jamie had a few minutes earlier.

SPENCE WAS SITTING on the side of his bed, staring blindly at the clenched fists dangling between his knees.

He wore nothing but his jeans, and his bare shoulders were slumped in a posture of pain that broke Libby's heart. She reacted to that pain as she did to any of her wounded patients—with a need to help that was stronger than any consideration of her own insecurities.

She sat on the bed beside him. "Spence?"

He shook his head. "I've let her down."

"Who? Jamie?"

He nodded.

"Don't be absurd. Jamie adores you. Spence, you're a wonderful father and Jamie is a secure, happy child."

"She was crying."

"Yes. She's also a normal child. She has her vulnerabilities, and her mother is one of them. But you saw how much she enjoyed herself at the theater this evening. She isn't suffering. She just needed a good cry tonight."

"*Damn* Delilah for hurting her like that," Spence exploded in quiet fury, his fist slamming down on his knee.

Libby covered his fist with her hand. "She hurt you, too."

"That isn't important," he muttered, shrugging off her sympathy. "Jamie's the one who matters."

"Not the only one." Libby wrapped her arm around him and brushed her lips across his cheek. "You matter, too, Spence. You matter very much."

He averted his face. "Libby, I—I'm not feeling quite in control tonight. Hell, I don't know what I'm feeling tonight."

"I know."

"I don't want to hurt you."

She smiled. Even in his own pain he thought of her. It was a start.

She pressed a kiss on his ear and stroked a hand down his bare chest. "Let me be here for you tonight, Spence. Let me take away the pain—at least for tonight."

She heard him swallow noisily when her hand slid across his stomach. She felt the quiver that ran through him. And she smiled. "I love you, Spence," she murmured, nibbling a kiss on his bottom lip. "Just let me love you tonight."

"Libby," he groaned. But he wasn't pushing her away.

She let her robe slide off her shoulders. And then she swept the cotton nightgown over her head. He wasn't looking away from her now, she saw in satisfaction.

She took his hand and lifted it to her right breast. "You don't really want me to leave, do you?"

His fingers twitched, then flexed. "No," he admitted. And then he said it again. "No. But—"

"Shut up, Spence," she whispered lovingly, her mouth only a breath away from his. And then her lips were on his, smothering any further arguments had he been inclined to make them.

Spence stopped fighting her. With a low growl of surrender, he pulled her into his bed, and into his arms.

12

THEY SAT IN THE second row of the huge Grand Palace theater—Gran on the inside, then Libby, then Jamie, and Spence in the aisle seat. Sylvia had spared no efforts getting good seats for her friends, and had been visibly proud of her efforts. They wouldn't have hurt her by turning them down. But that wasn't the only reason they were here. Through unspoken agreement, they seemed to understand that this was something that had to be done. Something that had to be faced.

Gran had been told of the relationship between Spence and Jamie and the big star who would be performing for them. She'd been startled, and then worried. She kept touching Libby's arm as they sat in the slowly filling theater, waiting for the event to start.

Trying not to think about what the next couple of hours could be like, Libby occupied herself studying the theater. The shades of mauve-and-green decor. The elaborate magnolia-blossom medallions decorating the walls. The concession stands discreetly placed at either side of the football-field-sized stage. The huge projection screens overhead, which enlarged the acts on stage for the benefit of those sitting high in the nose-bleed section. They'd already roamed through the gift shops in the enormous lobby, admiring the signed Glenda Turley prints and sequined souvenir T-shirts for sale, the gleaming white grand piano that had been signed by dozens of stars who'd performed on this stage, the sweeping staircases leading up to the balcony.

And all the time Libby had smiled like a manic robot, doing her best to hide her fears and insecurities. Was Spence looking forward to seeing Delilah again? Would he be dazzled by her? Would she look out in the audience and see him and Jamie—and regret her action in leaving them? And then she glanced at Jamie out of the corner of her eye. The child was unusually quiet, her eyes trained on the emcee as though she were afraid to miss a word he said. Libby reached out and took Jamie's hand, noticing that the soft little fingers were cold. "Would you like some popcorn or a soft drink, Jamie?" she asked. "I'll go get you something if you want."

Jamie smiled. "No, thank you. I'm not hungry right now."

"Okay." Libby returned the smile with the first genuine one she'd managed in hours.

Jamie didn't release her hand.

A dramatic drumroll brought a hush over the audience. A flash of light was followed by a heavy billow of white smoke. When it cleared, Delilah Payton stood at center stage, the bright lights gleaming on her lush red hair and her sleek, glittering sequined gown that was slit to reveal one long, slender leg. The crowd exploded.

Libby sank into her seat, feeling incredibly dowdy in her dark green sweater and matching slacks. She stared at the breathtakingly beautiful singer who had already launched into one of her most popular hits, and couldn't help picturing Spence holding her, kissing her, loving her. Oh, God, how could Libby ever compete with a woman like this?

She looked at Spence. If the memories were haunting him, she couldn't tell from his expression. He looked calm, detached, even a bit bored. Yet Libby was fully aware that none of those descriptions applied.

Jamie's fingers tightened convulsively around Libby's. Libby took Jamie's hands in both of her own, and they sat that way through the entire two-hour show.

Delilah didn't stop for an intermission, was gone from the stage only long enough for lightning-fast changes of costume—from one stunningly low-cut, glittering gown to another. She sang with an enthusiasm that seemed to radiate from her body to infuse the entire crowd with her energy.

It was easy to see why the audiences loved her. On stage, she was warm and eager and laughing and electric. She didn't just perform for her money, she earned every penny of it—and no one could doubt that she enjoyed every minute. Her voice was strong, husky, magical, her stage presence awesome. The audience loved her—and she loved them in return.

Libby grew more depressed with each passing moment.

No wonder Spence had been unable to forget. What man wouldn't be in love with a woman like this?

And how could a woman who seemed this warm, this approachable, this darned *nice*, ever walk away from an adorable child like Jamie? How could any mother hurt her child that way?

Delilah made it a practice to meet with her fans after each show, to shake their hands and sign autographs. She did so this time, as well, sitting on the edge of the stage like down-home royalty, her smile easy and friendly and open.

"Let's go," Spence said when the first rush to the stage had passed through the aisle, giving them a clear path to the exit.

"Dad." Jamie caught his arm. "Could we talk to her?"

Libby nearly choked. Spence looked startled. "You want to talk to her?" he asked. "Now?"

Jamie nodded.

Spence laid a hand on his daughter's shoulder. "Why, Jamie?"

"I just thought I'd tell her it was a good show," Jamie said with a shrug. "But if you want to leave now, it's okay."

Libby could see the conflict in Spence's eyes. He wanted to go, but he didn't want to reject his child's request. She held her breath, having no idea what she wanted his decision to be.

Spence finally exhaled and shrugged. "Okay, kid. Let's get in line. But, well, don't expect too much, all right?"

Jamie patted his hand. "I know, Dad."

The mature little gesture and tone in which she'd spoken would have made Libby smile at any other time.

"Gran and I will wait here," she said, starting to sit back down.

Jamie caught her hand. "No. Go with us. Please."

Libby was no more immune to the request than Spence had been, and no more happy about it. "All right, Jamie. If that's what you want."

Delilah really did have a talent for working crowds, Libby observed as they waited in line. The singer chatted briefly but encouragingly with everyone who passed by, signing autographs, fielding fervent compliments, yet skillfully keeping the line moving with the help of a muscular employee, who stood protectively nearby.

Jamie approached her first, with Spence's hand still resting on her shoulder. Libby and Gran stood close behind them.

Delilah glanced at Jamie first. Her smile was bright, impersonal. "Hello. And what's your name?"

"Jamie," her child said just as clearly. "Jamie Spencer."

Delilah's face paled beneath the stage paint. Her brilliant blue eyes flew upward, focusing on Spence's face in obvious shock. "Oh," she whispered. "Oh, God."

Spence looked back at her without expression. "Hello, Delilah."

"Michael," Delilah managed, her voice a thin parody of the rich timbre that had earned her fame. "What are you—?"

"We came to see your show," Jamie said. "We're on vacation here. Dad and me and Libby and Gran," she listed all in the same breath, swinging an arm to indicate the little group. "We're staying at Sylvia's Inn— she's a friend of my gran's." She subtly stressed the "my."

"It was a good show," she added just a bit too casually. "Almost as good as the one we saw last night at Mel Tillis's theater."

Libby bit her lip against a sudden, inappropriate smile. So sweet little Jamie just couldn't resist getting in one swipe of her tiny little claws. Libby couldn't say she blamed the child. She wanted very much to inflict a few scars herself. Heaven only knew how many emotional scars Delilah had left behind her.

Delilah reached out a scarlet-tipped hand to touch Jamie's cheek. Her eyes had turned to liquid, their vivid blue color reminding Libby of tropical seas. "It's good to see you, Jamie. You're so beautiful."

Jamie stepped back, crowding close to her father's side, one hand reaching out to take Libby's. "Thank you. We have to go now."

Delilah paled even more. Her gaze lingered for a moment on Jamie's hand in Libby's, then lifted to Spence, her lower lip quivering. "Michael?" she said, her voice a husky whisper. "Why don't you come backstage? We—we should talk."

Spence looked at her for a long time. Standing so close to them, Libby could almost feel the tension surrounding them, thought she could almost see the silent communication passing between the couple who'd once shared a marriage bed. Who'd once promised to love each other for a lifetime. Who'd made such a beautiful child together.

She could almost feel her own heart break as she watched them. Whatever had once existed between Spence and Delilah had been powerful. Was it all still there, still as strong as it had been before? Did Libby have any chance of making him love her that way?

Spence finally spoke. His voice held no more expression than his face. "It's late. Jamie should be in bed. She just wanted to say hello while we were here."

"Michael—please."

Libby wondered in despair how any man could resist that voice, that look.

Spence managed, though she couldn't have guessed what the effort cost him, if anything. "Not this time," he said. "But congratulations on your success. I guess you've got everything you always wanted now."

"No," she whispered, looking back at Jamie. "Not everything."

"Hey!" someone shouted from behind them in line. "We want to see her, too. Quit holding up the line."

"I'm afraid you're going to have to move along, folks," the oversize man in a Delilah Payton T-shirt said, glancing warily from his emotional employer to the small group who'd apparently perturbed her.

"Goodbye, Delilah." Spence gave the woman one last, level look, then turned without looking back and led the way to the exit, that supportive hand still on his daughter's shoulder.

Libby found that she was trembling. She felt Gran reach out and take her arm. Gran's hand wasn't steady, either. There was no way either of them could have witnessed that scene without reacting to the barely suppressed pain and anger.

IT WAS ALMOST midnight when Spence let himself into Libby's room. She looked up from the chair she'd been sitting in, staring at a book she hadn't been able to read. She hadn't known whether to expect him tonight or not, hadn't even known whether she'd wanted him to come to her. Now she knew that she had wanted it. Badly.

She set the book aside. "How's Jamie?"

"Sleeping like a baby." He kept his voice quiet in deference to the hour, and to the others sleeping down the hall. He closed the bedroom door behind him. "I guess she just needed to get it out of her system."

"Yes, I suppose she did." But what about Spence? Had he got anything out of his system? Or was she here only as a second choice to Delilah? Libby twisted her hands in front of her, feeling plain and uninteresting in comparison to the memory of Delilah Payton.

She'd been so determined to fight for Spence's love— but, oh, how she'd underestimated her opponent!

She ran a hand through her practically cut, dark-blond curls and said, "Delilah was even more beautiful in person than she is on television."

She regretted the words as soon as they left her mouth. Would Spence think she was fishing for compliments?

He took a step closer. "Delilah *is* beautiful," he agreed. "Mostly on the outside."

He lifted his hands to frame Libby's face between his palms. "Lately," he said deeply, "I've come to realize that it's the beauty that lies inside a person that really matters. And when a guy is lucky enough to find a woman who's beautiful on the outside *and* the inside—a woman like you—well, he'd be a fool to walk away from her."

Libby's knees went weak. The words were so tempting, yet so hard, to believe. "Spence," she murmured. "I don't—"

"Shh." He placed a finger over her lips, then moved it so that he could kiss her. So tenderly, so lingeringly, that she was trembling long before it ended.

"Some people," he murmured, "are so dazzled by rhinestones and glitter that they can't appreciate the lasting value of real, pure gold. I'm not one of those people, Libby. Not now." He kissed her again.

She was clinging to him now, her eyes burning, her throat tight. Wanting so desperately... yet so desperately afraid. "Spence," she began again, her voice a mere whisper.

Again he silenced her with a kiss. "Sometimes talk just gets in the way," he murmured against her lips. "Sometimes it's a lot more important to show than to tell."

She might have tried one more time to initiate a real conversation—about Delilah, about Jamie, about the future. Spence gave her no opportunity. His mouth covered hers again, and his hands began to move, and within minutes he'd swept away all coherent thought, all ability to speak lucidly.

He made love to her so thoroughly, so passionately, that she was little more than a puddle of quivering nerve endings by the time he finished.

And then he began again.

Sometime later she fell into an exhausted sleep, their bodies still joined, damp skin still fused. She woke only once during the night, briefly, groggily. Spence hadn't left her, hadn't gone back to his own bed. But he wasn't asleep. She sensed that he was lying awake, staring at the darkened ceiling.

Was he thinking about Delilah?

Libby closed her eyes and willed herself back to sleep. They would talk tomorrow, she thought hazily, wanting to cling to the remnants of pleasure for just a few more short hours. Desperately afraid of what tomorrow's talk would reveal.

THEY WERE JUST finishing breakfast the next morning when the inn's doorbell rang. Sylvia excused herself to go answer it, leaving the others to make their plans for their last day in Branson. They would be leaving that afternoon. Even Jamie seemed ready to go now, though she reiterated several times that she'd had a wonderful time on their vacation. Spence watched his daughter's face, searching for signs of distress and finding blessedly few. Jamie was happy to be having breakfast with her father and Libby and Gran, the people she loved most. She would always bear scars from being rejected by her mother, but Spence intended to make sure the remainder of her childhood was a happy one.

There'd been no opportunity so far for Spence and Libby to talk in private. He'd slipped out of her bed at daybreak, wanting to spare her the embarrassment of being discovered by his daughter or Libby's grandmother.

It had been very hard to leave her. He'd stood beside the bed for a long time, watching her sleep, seeing the fleeting smiles crossing her face and knowing she dreamed of him. He'd wanted nothing more than to crawl back in beside her and make those dreams reality again.

Sylvia appeared in the dining room doorway, her plain round face wearing a bemused expression. "Spence? You and Jamie have a visitor," she said, looking at him with dazed eyes. "She's waiting in the front parlor."

Jamie dropped her fork and looked at her father. He met her eyes, seeing the startled awareness there. Both of them knew who was calling.

"Damn," Spence muttered. And then he sighed. He guessed this was inevitable. Might as well get it over with. He dropped his napkin on the table and stood. "Come on, Jamie. You, too, Libby."

Libby stared, her face going pale. "Oh, no. I'll wait here with Gran and Sylvia. You go ahead."

Spence crossed his arms over his chest and stood without moving, just looking at her.

Libby shook her head. "I don't belong in there. This is between the three of you."

He tapped his booted foot on the polished hardwood floor.

"I think you'd better come with us, Libby," Jamie advised in a stage whisper. "When he gets that look on his face, there's just no arguing with him."

Libby reluctantly rose from her chair. "All right. But leave me out of it, will you?"

He took her arm and Jamie's hand and led both of them to the front parlor. Neither went along with a great deal of enthusiasm, he noticed with a faint ripple of amusement, watching out of the corner of his eye as Libby stiffly smoothed the red-and-white sweater she wore with slim black jeans. He could have told her she looked beautiful—fresh, natural, utterly, unselfconsciously sexy. He didn't. He figured he had plenty of time to convince her of that later.

Delilah wore a sweater, too—a thin black knit that glittered with sequined flower appliqués and clung revealingly to her full breasts. Her black knit slacks looked as though they'd been spray painted to her long, shapely legs. She'd probably spent a couple of hours on her teased and fluffed hair and perfectly applied makeup. Spence knew from experience that she had always spent a great deal of time on her appearance.

"Jamie!" Delilah rushed toward them, her arms reaching for the child. "Oh, Jamie. It's so wonderful to see you."

Jamie didn't pull away, but she didn't return the smothering hug, either. She gave Spence a wry look over Delilah's shoulder. He shot her a bracing grin in reply. Damn, but she was a great kid, he thought on a surge of pride. And Delilah had had little, if anything, to do with that—at least, not for the past five years.

Delilah wasn't the only one with something to show for those years. After doubting himself and his value for so long, the realization was a rather heady one.

"I'm sorry I couldn't say more to you yesterday," Delilah said to Jamie, pulling back a little to touch the child's cheek. "But with all the crowds, and the surprise you'd given me by showing up out of the blue, I just didn't know what to say."

"I know," Jamie said. "That's okay. I really did enjoy the show."

"Did you, sweetie?" Delilah beamed with pleasure. "I'm so glad."

Spence could feel Libby tugging surreptitiously at her arm, trying to get him to release her. He knew she'd bolt the minute he let go. He tightened his fingers. "Delilah," he greeted his ex-wife. "We weren't expecting you this morning."

"I know," she said, straightening to look at Spence. "I had my driver find this place. He's waiting outside in the limo," she added casually.

Spence only nodded. Did she ever think back to the shabby little rooms they'd shared? The cheap meals they'd eaten? He hoped if she did, there were some good memories mixed in with the bad. He'd spent the past five years dwelling too deeply on the bad, which hadn't been entirely fair to either of them.

He couldn't help noticing that Delilah was trying not to look at Libby. She'd always had a knack for ignoring what she didn't want to deal with, he remembered. But he wouldn't let her get away with it this time.

He drew Libby forward, easily overcoming her token resistance. "We never got around to introductions yesterday, did we? Libby, this is Delilah Payton. Delilah, I'd like you to meet Dr. Libby Carter."

"Doctor?" Delilah repeated, lifting a perfectly arched brow.

"I'm a veterinarian," Libby explained, shooting Spence a chiding look. "It's very nice to meet you, Ms. Payton. I'm quite a fan of your music."

Spence wasn't surprised when Delilah's smile grew a bit more genuine. She'd always been a sucker for a compliment. She'd craved them the same way most people needed food and water.

"It's very nice to meet you, too, Dr. Carter," she said with practiced ease. Star to fan. Probably a much more comfortable role for her than ex-wife to new lover, Spence thought. "I wonder if you'd be kind enough to excuse us for a few minutes. I'd like to talk to my husband and my daughter for a bit in private."

"No," Spence broke in when Libby automatically started to agree. "Libby stays."

Delilah's brow rose higher. Her voice was amused. "Honestly, Michael, one would think you were afraid to be alone with me."

"No," he said with a shrug. "I just don't see any reason for it."

She pouted. He could remember a time when her pouts had turned him inside out. "But, Michael. There are some things I really need to say to you."

He inclined his head. "I have a few things to say to you, too, Delilah. And I want Libby to hear them."

"I, uh, think I'll go talk to Gran," Jamie announced, taking a step toward the doorway.

Spence winked at her. "Might be a good idea."

"Jamie, sweetheart, you don't have to leave," Delilah said, looking contrite that the child had been made to feel uncomfortable.

But Jamie only flashed a smile and skipped out.

Delilah sighed and turned back to Spence. "Oh, Michael," she said, laying a hand on his arm. "She's so beautiful." Her brilliant blue eyes gleamed with what might have been a film of tears.

"Yes. She's going to look very much like her mother."

That pleased her. Her eyelids drooped and her hand moved slowly on his arm. "She has a bit of her father in her, as well. You always were a very sexy man."

Libby shifted restlessly.

There'd been a time when Delilah could have looked at him like that and had his tongue hanging to his knees. He found it interesting—and damned refreshing—that he could acknowledge her sultry sexuality now without becoming entrapped in it.

"Oh, Michael." Delilah sighed delicately. "You wouldn't believe how many times I've thought of you and Jamie."

"No," he agreed. "I probably wouldn't."

She flinched. "I guess I should have expected that. I know how angry you were when I left. I'd hoped you'd learned to forgive me since then—at least a little."

"It wasn't just anger, Delilah."

She bit her lower lip. "I know," she whispered. "I hurt you. Both of you. And I've never stopped regretting it. Never. But—"

"But I didn't give you any other choice," Spence said with a slight sigh. "I forced you to choose—and you made the only choice you could live with."

It was the first time he'd admitted it to her, maybe the first time he'd admitted it to himself. All these years he'd hated Delilah for leaving, blamed her for abandoning him and Jamie. He still couldn't really understand how a woman could choose a career over her own child, but he knew now that Delilah couldn't have ever been happy with the sort of life he lived. He'd watched her on that stage yesterday, and he'd realized that she was truly happy, utterly fulfilled. She'd never looked quite like that before. The applause was her lifeblood, her adoring fans the only family she really needed.

The quiet, private, peaceful existence that made him happy would have slowly killed her—in spirit, if not in actuality. If she had stayed with Spence and Jamie, they would all have been miserable.

"Yes," Delilah agreed. "I had to leave. You've seen what was waiting for me, what I always knew was waiting for me. I tried to tell you then, begged you to go after it with me, but you would never listen. You never understood."

"You're right, Dee," he agreed, falling back into the nickname he'd called her. "You've finally gotten what you wanted. You always knew you'd get there some-day—and I doubted you. I was wrong."

"I've had to make a lot of sacrifices along the way," she said.

Her words triggered a flicker of the old anger. "You sure as hell sacrificed your marriage and your kid."

"I didn't want to," she whispered. "I wanted you to come with me. But you wouldn't. And I had to go. I couldn't have done what I had to do with Jamie to care for. I knew you'd take care of her, you always did. But I've missed her. And I've missed you, Michael."

She moved closer, subtly insinuating herself between Spence and Libby in an unconsciously self-centered move that was so very typical of single-minded Delilah. "It's gets very lonely on the road, Michael. Do you understand loneliness?"

"Yes," he said roughly, remembering all those long, painful nights. "I know loneliness."

"Maybe we don't have to be lonely anymore," she murmured. "You and Jamie can come with me. Now that I've made it, there's no reason we can't be together again. I can take care of all of us now."

Spence stared down at her. And realized that the moment he'd dreamed about for so many years had arrived. Delilah wanted him back. How many times had he fantasized about this? How many times—even recently—had he wondered what he'd do, what he'd say? All he had to do was say yes and Delilah would be his again. His and a couple million others.

He touched her face. "You know, Dee, if you'd made this offer a year ago—maybe even six months ago—I'd have been tempted to take you up on it. Maybe. But now, well, it's too late. You've found your life—and I've found mine."

Delilah's eyes widened, then turned from him to Libby. "I see," she murmured, and let her hand fall to her side.

Spence's mind filled with images. Libby on horseback, enjoying a crisp, quiet autumn afternoon. Libby with her grandmother, patient and loving and respectful. Libby with her blond curls bent soothingly over a crying child—Spence's crying child. The tenderness she'd shown Jamie, the passion she'd given to him. And he knew that he could never ask for anything—or anyone—else. He turned to smile at Libby, finding her watching him with huge, painfully vulnerable eyes.

"But, Michael—" Delilah was obviously not fully convinced that he could resist her. Wryly remembering what an idiot he'd been about her before, he couldn't exactly blame her for doubting his imperviousness now.

"We had some good times together, Dee," he acknowledged without looking away from Libby. "Some real good times. And we made ourselves one hell of a terrific kid. But it's been over a long time. You've got what you wanted. Fame, money, glamour, an exciting life on the road. You always needed a lot more love than Jamie and I could give you, and you've got it now. The whole damned world loves you. But I need something different. One man, one very special woman.

"I need a family," he said, speaking only to Libby now. "A real home. And I've been lucky enough to find that. If she'll have me."

Delilah had no choice but to concede defeat, but she clung proudly to her dignity. Her chin held high, she stepped back. "Well," she said, little emotion on her beautiful face. "I suppose I should congratulate you."

"I hope so," Spence murmured, still looking at Libby.

"Well." Delilah smoothed the hem of her sweater so that it stretched even more tightly over her breasts. "I'd better be going. I have a matinee to do this afternoon."

"Good luck with it."

"Thank you. Um, do you need any money or anything? For Jamie, I mean."

Spence bit back the quick flash of temper, knowing Delilah had been unable to resist her own subtle revenge. "No, Delilah. I don't need any money. Jamie and I are getting along just fine."

"Maybe she could come visit me this summer. I'll be on tour, of course, but she could come along. She'll have a great time. I—"

"No." Spence spoke sharply this time, wanting to make himself perfectly clear. "You walked away from Jamie five years ago, and you haven't even bothered to send her a birthday card since. Maybe you thought it was best, maybe you thought it would make it easier for all of us. But she's mine, Delilah. You want to fight it out in court, we'll do so, but you better be prepared for one hell of a dirty fight."

"You would keep her away from her own mother?" Delilah demanded.

"I won't stop you from writing or calling her. And you can see her any time you want to stop by Little Rock—that's where we're living now. But I'll be damned if I'm sending a little girl on the road with you, to be looked after by nannies and stage managers until you have a few minutes to spend with her between performances and appearances."

"Does this mean you've stopped dragging her along with you on the rodeo circuit?"

He winced inwardly at the direct hit, but kept his expression calm. "I've retired from the rodeo," he announced, and heard Libby's small gasp of reaction. "I've got a little money coming and I'm starting my own business raising and training rodeo horses. I won't ever get rich at it, but you know that was never one of *my* priorities. I'll send you an address in case you ever want to drop Jamie a line. I won't advise her to hold her breath, of course. You've always known how to get in touch with us, one way or another."

Delilah's face was pale beneath the rouge. "I won't fight you for her, Spence. You know as well as I do that I'd only be hurting myself, that the public would never understand what I had to do five years ago. But I hope you don't regret this someday. I hope Jamie doesn't resent that you deprived her of this."

"Jamie doesn't feel deprived of anything," Spence returned. "She has a nice home, a full-time father and a family who loves her. She's making all As in school, she's learning to knit—she's even got her own cat. She's doing just fine, Delilah."

"I'm glad," Delilah said, and the anger had receded enough to show the sincerity in her eyes. "You always were a good father to her, Michael. It's obvious that she adores you. I just hope that someday she'll be able to forgive me."

He nodded. "I've never said a bad word about you to her, Dee. She knows you did what you felt you had to do. It hurts her, but she doesn't hate you. I've never wanted her to."

"Thank you for that." She turned to Libby and extended her hand. "Goodbye, Dr. Carter. Take good care of them."

"I'll certainly do my best," Libby answered, the first time she'd spoken since she'd been introduced to the other woman. Spence was proud of the way she held her head up and met Delilah eye to eye. He didn't want Libby to ever again feel inferior to Delilah—or anyone else, for that matter.

Maybe he didn't deserve her, but now that he'd found her, now that she'd been foolish enough to fall in love with him, he intended to spend the rest of his life proving himself worthy of that love.

"Kiss Jamie goodbye for me, Michael," Delilah said, turning toward the door. "I think that would be easier for—for all of us."

Spence would never know if the touching little break in her voice had been real, or feigned. He wanted to believe, for Jamie's sake and for Delilah's, that it had been real.

He turned back to Libby the moment Delilah had swept dramatically away. She stood in the center of the room, pale and nervous, her hands twisting in front of her. They both heard the front door close, listened to the sound of the limo's engine fading down the street.

It was Libby who broke the silence. "She's gone."

"Yes." And this time it had been his choice. Damn, but it felt good. He took a step toward Libby, reaching for her. "Libby—"

She turned away, evading his arms. He let them fall to his sides. "What's wrong?"

Her head was down, her fingers twisted so tightly the knuckles were white. "I—I think we should give this a little time."

"You mean us? Our relationship?" he clarified.

"Yes." She spoke in a whisper, barely loud enough for him to hear. "I think it would be best."

"You said you love me," he reminded her, his stomach clenching. "Are you telling me that you aren't sure about that now? That you've changed your mind?"

"No," she choked.

"No *what*, damn it?"

"I haven't changed my mind. I love you, Spence. I have almost from the start. But you—"

He felt the knotted muscles in his neck begin to relax. "What about me?"

She took a deep breath. "I don't want to be your second choice," she burst out, finally looking straight at him. "I don't want to be married because I come complete with a nice home and a grandmother for Jamie. I don't want to feel that I have to always compete with a memory. I need more than that, damn it."

"And you have it," he said, dropping his hands on her shoulders. "You don't have to compete with anyone, Libby Carter. You're the most special woman I've ever known. If I hadn't been such a hardheaded jerk, I'd have admitted that I loved you weeks ago. I did then—and I do now. I love you, Libby. You aren't my second choice. You're my first. For now, for always."

Libby caught her breath and looked up at him with an expression of hope and longing that tore him apart. He caught her in his arms. "I used to be a certified fool, Libby. Don't hold that against me now. I know the difference now between glitter and real gold. Delilah's the glitter—and so is that damned rodeo buckle I've been chasing to help me get over her. You're the gold. And Jamie, and Gran, and the rest of the family we're going to make together. What man in his right mind would throw that away for a handful of rhinestones and sequins?"

"Delilah's so beautiful," she whispered, her eyelids going heavy when he brushed his lips against her cheek.

"So are you," he murmured, touching his mouth to each of the five freckles on her adorable nose. "And it doesn't take you two hours with paint and hair spray to get that way."

Her hands lifted to his chest, then curled around his shoulders. "I work too hard. Spend too many hours at the clinic."

"Yeah. We'll have to change that. You can have a successful practice without endangering your health or neglecting your family. Other women do, as you reminded me once before."

"Yes." She returned the light, gentle kiss he gave her. "Spence?" she whispered when he lifted his head an inch or so.

"Yeah?"

"You really love me?"

"I love you," he growled, punctuating the words with another longer, deeper kiss. "I love you. I'm going to spend the rest of my life proving it to you."

"I'm going to hold you to that," she whispered, and then threw herself against him. "Oh, Spence. I love you. And I want very much to make a family with you."

He hugged her against him, resisting a crazy impulse to throw both arms in the air and whoop with victory. This was the prize he'd been chasing after for most of his life, he realized. This was the gold.

Looked as if Michael Spencer was a real winner, after all.

COMING NEXT MONTH

#505 EVEN COWBOYS GET THE BLUES Carin Rafferty
Lost Loves, Book 5

No *way* would Annie O'Neill ever work with her lying and cheating ex-husband again. So what if Tanner Chapel needed her to help write his country songs? So what if he claimed he wasn't so bad? So what if he was still the sexiest damn cowboy she'd *ever* laid eyes on?

#506 SCANDALS JoAnn Ross

One night of fiery passion changed the lives of Bram Fortune and Dani Cantrell forever. Grieving over the death of Bram's brother, who was also her fiancé, Dani had turned to Bram. Six weeks later Dani learned she was pregnant. Bram insisted they marry...but would Dani ever stop loving his brother?

#507 PLAIN JANE'S MAN Kristine Rolofson

Plain Jane won a man. Well, not *exactly*. Jane Plainfield won a boat and gorgeous Peter Johnson came with it. Jane hated the water, so what was she going to do with the boat? Even worse, she had been badly burned by romance—so what was she going to do with the man? Especially when he wouldn't take *no* for an answer?

#508 STAR Janice Kaiser

Five years ago, Hollywood lured rising star Dina Winters. She landed a movie deal, but left fiancé Michael Cross at the altar. Now hotshot director Michael wants Dina for *his* movie. But she'll need an Oscar-winning performance to work with the sexy man she never stopped loving....

MILLION DOLLAR SWEEPSTAKES (III)

No purchase necessary. To enter, follow the directions published. Method of entry may vary. For eligibility, entries must be received no later than March 31, 1996. No liability is assumed for printing errors, lost, late or misdirected entries. Odds of winning are determined by the number of eligible entries distributed and received. Prizewinners will be determined no later than June 30, 1996.

Sweepstakes open to residents of the U.S. (except Puerto Rico), Canada, Europe and Taiwan who are 18 years of age or older. All applicable laws and regulations apply. Sweepstakes offer void wherever prohibited by law. Values of all prizes are in U.S. currency. This sweepstakes is presented by Torstar Corp., its subsidiaries and affiliates, in conjunction with book, merchandise and/or product offerings. For a copy of the Official Rules send a self-addressed, stamped envelope (WA residents need not affix return postage) to: MILLION DOLLAR SWEEPSTAKES (III) Rules, P.O. Box 4573, Blair, NE 68009, USA.

EXTRA BONUS PRIZE DRAWING

No purchase necessary. The Extra Bonus Prize will be awarded in a random drawing to be conducted no later than 5/30/96 from among all entries received. To qualify, entries must be received by 3/31/96 and comply with published directions. Drawing open to residents of the U.S. (except Puerto Rico), Canada, Europe and Taiwan who are 18 years of age or older. All applicable laws and regulations apply; offer void wherever prohibited by law. Odds of winning are dependent upon number of eligible entries received. Prize is valued in U.S. currency. The offer is presented by Torstar Corp., its subsidiaries and affiliates in conjunction with book, merchandise and/or product offering. For a copy of the Official Rules governing this sweepstakes, send a self-addressed, stamped envelope (WA residents need not affix return postage) to: Extra Bonus Prize Drawing Rules, P.O. Box 4590, Blair, NE 68009, USA.

SWP-H894

HARLEQUIN®
Temptation

Lost Loves

RIGHT MAN...WRONG TIME

Remember that one man who turned your world upside down? Who made you experience all the ecstatic highs of passion and lows of loss and regret. What if you met him again?

You dared to lose your heart once and had it broken. Dare you love again?

JoAnn Ross, Glenda Sanders, Rita Clay Estrada, Gina Wilkins and Carin Rafferty. Find their stories in Lost Loves, Temptation's newest miniseries, running May to September 1994.

In September, experience EVEN COWBOYS GET THE BLUES by Carin Rafferty. A one-night stand had cost country-western hotshot Tanner Chapel plenty. His marriage with Annie was over, his career was on the skids and his dreams had begun to die. He wanted Annie back...but could she learn to love and trust again?

What if...?

LOST5

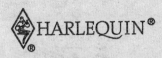

HARLEQUIN®

Weddings, Inc.

THE WEDDING GAMBLE
Muriel Jensen

Eternity, Massachusetts, was America's wedding town. Paul Bertrand knew this better than anyone—he never should have gotten soused at his friend's rowdy bachelor party. Next morning when he woke up, he found he'd somehow managed to say "I do"—to the woman he'd once jilted! And Christina Bowman had helped launch so many honeymoons, she knew just what to do on theirs!

THE WEDDING GAMBLE, available in September from American Romance, is the fourth book in Harlequin's new cross-line series, **WEDDINGS, INC.**

Be sure to look for the fifth book, **THE VENGEFUL GROOM,** by Sara Wood (Harlequin Presents #1692), coming in October.

WED4

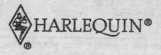

HARLEQUIN®

Don't miss these Harlequin favorites by some of our most distinguished authors!
And now you can receive a discount by ordering two or more titles!

HT #25525	THE PERFECT HUSBAND by Kristine Rolofson	$2.99 ☐
HT #25554	LOVERS' SECRETS by Glenda Sanders	$2.99 ☐
HP #11577	THE STONE PRINCESS by Robyn Donald	$2.99 ☐
HP #11554	SECRET ADMIRER by Susan Napier	$2.99 ☐
HR #03277	THE LADY AND THE TOMCAT by Bethany Campbell	$2.99 ☐
HR #03283	FOREIGN AFFAIR by Eva Rutland	$2.99 ☐
HS #70529	KEEPING CHRISTMAS by Marisa Carroll	$3.39 ☐
HS #70578	THE LAST BUCCANEER by Lynn Erickson	$3.50 ☐
HI #22256	THRICE FAMILIAR by Caroline Burnes	$2.99 ☐
HI #22238	PRESUMED GUILTY by Tess Gerritsen	$2.99 ☐
HAR #16496	OH, YOU BEAUTIFUL DOLL by Judith Arnold	$3.50 ☐
HAR #16510	WED AGAIN by Elda Minger	$3.50 ☐
HH #28719	RACHEL by Lynda Trent	$3.99 ☐
HH #28795	PIECES OF SKY by Marianne Willman	$3.99 ☐

Harlequin Promotional Titles

#97122	LINGERING SHADOWS by Penny Jordan	$5.99 ☐
	(limited quantities available on certain titles)	

	AMOUNT	$
DEDUCT:	10% DISCOUNT FOR 2+ BOOKS	$
	POSTAGE & HANDLING	$
	($1.00 for one book, 50¢ for each additional)	
	APPLICABLE TAXES*	$_____
	TOTAL PAYABLE	$_____
	(check or money order—please do not send cash)	

To order, complete this form and send it, along with a check or money order for the total above, payable to Harlequin Books, to: **In the U.S.:** 3010 Walden Avenue, P.O. Box 9047, Buffalo, NY 14269-9047; **In Canada:** P.O. Box 613, Fort Erie, Ontario, L2A 5X3.

Name: _____

Address:_____City: _____

State/Prov.: _____ Zip/Postal Code: _____

*New York residents remit applicable sales taxes.
 Canadian residents remit applicable GST and provincial taxes..